Qurratulain

By James Chapman

Our Plague: A Film from New York

The Walls Collide as You Expand, Dwarf Maple

Glass (Pray the Electrons Back to Sand)

In Candyland It's Cool to Feed on Your Friends

Daughter! I Forbid Your Recurring Dream!

Stet

How Is This Going to Continue?

Degenerescence

The Rat Veda

Qurratulain

James Chapman

fugue state press
new york

ISBN 978-1-879193-26-0

Library of Congress Control Number: 2012933134

Front cover: Holy Mary of Egypt. 18th century icon,
Kuopio Orthodox Church Museum

Back cover: Geb, Nut, and Shu

A fragment of this novel first appeared in
Review of Contemporary Fiction

Fugue State Press
PO Box 80, Cooper Station
New York NY 10276

www.fuguestatepress.com
jim@fuguestatepress.com

to carah

everything

Qurratulain

Apart from those who dwelt as monks in Egypt's desert, there was also in that era a man of God called Spek who lived in the center of a seaside town as if he were cloistered. He never left the walls of his small stone chapel, but worshiped bright Creation from darkness.

With him dwelt only the bishop called Nonnus, and this is not the Nonnus of beloved memory. This Nonnus was one who fell into doctrinal error in Armenia, and was removed to this unimportant place, to become reestablished in the faith and to pray for deliverance, especially from anger.

Now when this town's pagan festival of the Exaltation of Flowers came around, these two men avoided looking out of doors that entire week, so as to avoid the sight of processions and profane celebration. But Satan having played the people of this town as if they were the psaltery he fiddles upon, then there was peace on the Monday, and both men stood near the open door in the brightness of that summer afternoon.

Along the empty street there now walked a woman named Qurratulain. She was recently arrived of India or Persia, or may have been of another land. Some who saw her said she was above thirty years, others said she was as young as sixteen.

She was dressed in a single garment, which if witnesses were all correct was of every color and material, and it seemed to gather around her like a cloud, clinging to her out of desire. Her untamed hair flowed out like the oldest carvings of Nile queens, black as onyx and curling in a thousand spiral strands. Her bare feet seemed powdered with pearls.

So great was her beauty that the breezes of the city stopped blowing, and the paving stones seemed to hold their breath. There was no path to her that did not end in beauty. By seeing her dark eyes, you could scent feathers and sunlight.

As she walked, she looked one time through the open church door. Then she walked on.

Bishop Nommus hid his face from her. The priest named Spek, however, stood gazing after her as she walked away.

Black doves flew around the rafters of the church, and Spek was unable to speak. The doves gathered around him, settling on his shoulders and head, yet he did not perceive them there.

Then a citizen of the town came running to the church, saying, "Fathers, the woman Qurratulain who just passed by has fallen in the street, and is tearing her clothing and weeping and calling out in tongues unknown to us."

Spek stepped outside, into the direct light of the sun.

✝

Before I saw her, I prayed to a god without a name, called plain "God," and he had no mother and no wife. No mother, no wife. No mother and no wife.

Before I saw her, I watched the street outside this church and said the following prayer to the god God:

Lord, because you're a demanding father who expects divine indifference of us, you created these dancing girls who loll their bodies on the stone steps, and drape themselves in doorways, and know how not to look at me so I'll be free to look at them as long as I want. You created the young men who walk pouting their mouths, making their faces into waterfalls of beauty. You created maidens who pass with their faces turned to the left but eyes rolled to the right, as if watching a bee, just to create unguarded beauty in the face.

Lord God: you created the flower in its brief irresistible perfection. Then you told us to hate the flower, told us a flower is without meaning.

Today as I stood watching the city from your door, I prayed with love and gratitude to your son Jesus, thanking him for being permanent among this evanescence. I held his presence pressed into the hollow of my chest. As dozens of women passed me on the footpath, I felt my skin seethe, yet Jesus without anger explained to me the emptiness of these faces, the lack in their hearts, the inability of a flower to understand death or eternity. Lord God: I swallow my entire mammal self, I try to adore death and eternity, I gaze at the placid face of your son who does not desire. I let the enormous sky-spanning stone of you, God, fall upon me. I crush my sex against stone, and shudder.

Lord God: when you came to earth to walk in the garden, did you look on Eve's body knowing she couldn't understand the beauty you'd put there?

Lord God: when you impregnated Mary, did you intertwine her soul in the night till her core trembled and became like silver in the furnace? Did she flow toward you like light through water, and vanish into you like the desperate lost hours of a human girl who was born to be forgotten, and who never did worship the flesh, never knew about the world?

She loved you for the gesture and the presence without words or names, and there was not even joy because joy is one thing and you are all. Did she never ask you a single question? Not even to find out if you only chose her for her beauty?

"Lord, my mind is a grain of salt on the seashore, I will be dissolved in the next tide. Your mind is the whole ocean. You could take any woman of this world. Creator of the universe, what have you done? You're too immense. I'm thrashing, terrorized, mute, weeping. Why are you reaching into me?"

Qurratulain came into this world through the sex of a woman. She was many different ages when I saw her. For sixteen years I had worshiped the purity of the desolated Jesus.

The day I saw her, I already knew her. Those sixteen years she'd prayed into the heart of earth from morning to night, creating me from nothing. She, who created the world, she stepped into the world and devoted herself to me. She spoke this way, and I heard it:

Beloved, I came to earth again, this time to a city of yearning. I came to find you. My skin was so new it absorbed the beauty of every face. I glowed with the desires of all humans. The earth was flesh, begging the sky to press against it.

Human flesh feet padded along every sidewalk, imprinting heat so tender it softened the stones.

Each flesh face was a world held in orbit by need.

I'm here. I hold the long spoon that stirs skin and need into each other. I need to stir you so deep into my liquid world that even sunlight is a thick cream inside us.

In the envelope of a plain girl I've walked here for years, loving every face. But if I spoke—if I came up to one of these glowing men or women, and said to them, "You," they became small again, skittish mammals biting at clumps of their own fur.

So I would gaze and not speak.

Some days beauty would rise and re-exalt itself until it vibrated unbearably.

People who passed me were filled with the remains of the old gods. So many suns, oceans, rivers passed me in the streets of your city, so many winds and flames, There is Diana and there, and there. There is Seshat whose body is poetry, stretching the white cord within herself. None of the beautiful strollers knew their power; they didn't know that if they would press their foreheads to my belly, with their fingers inside me, they could steer the ship of the universe.

I'm every woman today, I'm every fragrant wine. I'm coming for you.

Your eyelashes flicker against the skin of my name.

Your ears are milk, aching to be churned by my name.

My joy pours into you, like the joy of crawling into the body of the beloved.

The creator within me poured her creation into me, and I filled with our universe as I walked along. I was overflowing honey and amber and liquid jewels of the goddess who makes the core of her body into words that lick our lips.

When you look at the human world through sheets of honey, everything is sweet amber flesh, shimmering heat for our bodies to bake in.

In love trance I walked, my feet took me to the small stone fortress you inhabit. In the door was a human face, a pair of eyes that can love endlessly, as they all can. As always I wanted to stretch out my arms, kiss, give, pour myself, I had everything to pour.

But this time the face was yours.

You saw my eyes through to the bottoms of my feet.

A Christian X was on your door. The black air of the church, saturated with love in mummy form, love bandaged into duty, that dark air poured out the door around your body. In my short life on earth I'd already loved men and women, and some were Christians. So I knew about Christians. So I was afraid you'd be frightened, easily angered. I thought you'd hate me and beat me with that god if I spoke to you.

I looked away, but from my hip to my throat I felt the sun enter me. It had been waiting.

I felt you watching me. You watched me like plowing circles into the earth to confuse all the rivers.

You watched me like stroking my body with all the stars.

You spread a field out against the sky. I don't think I was walking anymore. You populated the sky with banners, honeycombs, white lights, you spread marigolds and honeysuckle on the dome, you made an earth that was not on earth.

You made an earth that was already loved by the sky, you made an earth that lay in the arms of the sky.

Your eyes were blue sky, you curled them around my brown eyes.

You stood naked, your skin so pale it hurt me.

You stepped outside your church fortress. You gathered me onto a pillar of cloud you billowed out, a curved cloud like you'd drawn one of my eyebrows in white.

The sky pouring its entire self into me.

The sky collapsing into me, into me.

You curled over me as the sky embraces the earth, like air wraps a drop of water. You surrounded every bit of me, touching without harm, holding without effort, but eternally.

My thighs were bound up by your eyes. Milk spilled from my breasts and wet my belly.

You looked at my shining belly and closed your eyes.

The pain of love. I'd only seen that pain in myself.

You who held me in your eyes gently, held me furiously.

Not yet taking ownership of my skin, instead you gripped my blood. In your two eyes you showed me our two children.

In my arms writhed two creatures smaller than the gods of waterdrops, more pale than the sun at the center of my body, more aflame than the tiny gap of air between my skin and yours.

They were us. They were the clay gods of us.

My beloved, my one beloved. You weighed a million pounds from a stone church in your throat, but your body popped like a bubble when you saw my eyes.

You lived all your life without a mouth, and yet sang love with a breath that never stopped.

You knelt to your Lord without legs, yet ran to me when you discovered my face.

You're long and tall, but you walked my skin for miles without turning.

You're orderly in your ways, but forgot to map my body as you explored it.

You were born with a compass in your mind, but got lost forever in my hair.

You knelt in my skin and prayed to me.

You said:

Forgive me   I disregarded your footsteps on the earth   I knew for fact you couldn't exist.   Oh courier of dreams   Who walks at night and changes my breath in dreams   I knew you as a vacancy   I felt the empty shape of you, all my life   Knew your voice, knew your mouth , and the place your face would rest against my chest   For decades I walked with you in front of me The absence of you pulled me forward   I wanted to swallow this vacuum Now you step into the space before my chest   You push out the sky, you destroy the earth   You destroy heaven and time   You destroy PERFECT mosaics of proof, and beautifully planed and joined faith   YOU DESTROY GOD

Spek, beloved, your prayer stopped suddenly, just there.

God of Spek, do prayers to you suddenly stop in fear?

On the god-soaked earth, this translucent man made himself invisible decades ago.

He loved and loved, and love was only thirst.

He was desolated, yearning to be touched, but alone in the world.

He was ripe for you, Lord.

He was the fruit that throws itself from the tree. He was the ritual center of your cult. His core belongs to my hand, but you took him with your talk of the least, the humble, the mocked, as you invite the despised and rejected into your religion of needy castoffs and residue.

He was an easy recruit, begging to hand himself over.

He gave himself, and his infinite love pressed angels out of your breath. Before I was even born he was fuel for your flame. But the day I was born onto your planet, I cried for his arms. My husband was staring at a picture of your son that day, willing himself to feel filled. He didn't know yet that he was lying across my belly.

The day I was born, my womb was already hidden under his tongue. One of us, you or me, Lord, was poison to his heart. My absence or yours.

His love was too strong for your heaven. You never allowed him to ignite, he would have usurped the sun.

In the body all women have, I walked past a stone house where your son Jesus was displayed tortured in effigy, naked with the beauty all men have.

Inside was the a man chosen by pride, a bishop who did not say no to robes and honors, and with him my husband, who also called himself married to the church, but whose body shrank from wearing a robe or ring.

His name was Spek, this is the small sound your world has pressed like clay into my ears. In the night, pale orange words glowed below his ribs. The bishop would hover over my husband in his sleep, trying to read him.

The words would change every minute, in lettering no one knew. Like the marks you leave on old stones in this land, Lord.

The bishop would transcribe every letter, and show the writing to Spek in the morning as if blaming him, and Spek felt the meaning but didn't know a true way to speak of it. His knowledge embarrassed him.

The bishop would command him to stop glowing, to be more perfect than the sun, more blameless than a stone, more strong than a need, more passionless than a noose.

God, the raw hearts you create in your image, and the harsh hot-eyed soldiers. You feel everything we feel. You yearn since we do. You're as arrogant as we are.

In the night, alone, that bishop would tremble at the infinite intensity of your creation, Lord, at the fatal beauty of the mammal body, at the pull of the entire earth at the sex of man. And he would try to die to you, to crush his innate flame under a mountain. As you showed him beauty, he would show you his conquest of beauty.

To the bishop, Lord, you were a correct sum. You were truth as the opposite of error. Knowing the answer gave him no joy, because joy would have carried him *away from his sums into the arms of angels.*

Angels are tall perfect bodies with wings that can wrap and hold. Oh we need them.

To my husband whose belly speaks in colored writing, my man who won't say an untrue thing, and so hardly speaks—to him, joy was complete and frozen. Joy was waiting all those years, numb in his chest.

He writhed with the need to melt it, but you told him no.

Lord, because we have bodies, you feel your body.

My husband couldn't love you, but only serve you. He waited to love you joyfully.

You were too stern, and he turned to your dead son. He wanted a path to you. He sang in Christ's heart, to try to hear your answering song.

Then stopped in the corridor and stared at the stone ceiling for minutes. He realized Jesus never sang.

When you said This is my son, in whom I am well-pleased, *Spek gasped. He wanted to be praised like a son.*

When he read your son's words to you, The world knows that you have loved them, as you have loved me, *Spek closed his eyes. Here was proof. He waited to feel your joy in him.*

Eyes shut, he saw burning.

From the soles of his feet to the ends of his hair he was desolate, the infinite paths in him were empty. The cities in him were burnt, they were waste. The earth in him was devoured by strangers who consumed his land with their mouths.

Eyes shut he saw the whole planet of his mind wounded and bruised with age, with waiting.

He saw the whole planet of his heart, and it was faint and thin, ill.

He saw the distant cold sun. A painted sun, a smudge.

But Lord, father god, he didn't know your heart. Upon your finger, I have wrapped myself. I kiss you constantly.

Lord God, I make your belly twist upon itself. I set a haze before your eyes, Lord.

The planet fire is my voice in your ear. The volcano, that is me touching your skin.

I pour back all that your loneliness takes away. I give more than you ever created. I live at your finger, and in the light of the sun. My low voice turns the planets.

I'm small, and my hair fills the firmament, and my eyes swallow the galaxies, my voice is the throne you writhe on.

I'm a little ring on your finger, worth all the treasure in your creation.

I'm here as a human girl, my treasure is the instant of my smile, the sudden gesture of my fingers. This flashing vanishing is the beauty.

You created a world that glows and disappears, to express your heart.

The bishop and his priest Spek, in their despair they give over to you, and you flood them with more despair, so they see beauty in a flowing easy death. Looking for despair, they have come to the source.

What you do is simple. They ask, and you're silent.

All they would need would be to see your ring, and touch your ring. Why won't you give away your secret?

Here, these two worshippers you made. You disappointed and frightened them, year by year, till they grasped each other's hands in terror.

They made a church out of your silence. Stone for the walls, because stone is like you. They molded peace out of your absence.

They'll try to drink love out of any cup you give them. You gave them the awareness of death, and they thanked you. They even turned death into a wonderland, a vast vacation from work, from emptiness, from itching. Even though you know your creatures die and crumble into the earth. You secretly know their souls just go out, as softly as small lamps.

The heaven they created was need. It desired you, it sang your praise desperately so you would sit almost within reach.

The bishop and his priest felt like servants in your heaven. They knew they'd better praise you loudly or you'd send them away.

They dreamed, hoping they'd want to love you.

On earth, in life, they tried to love you, but you make it so hard, petulant Lord, cruel child-god.

When they were young, these two men looked out into the world and saw a place that had already cut them into segments.

They were unbelievers, the way Moses was. They couldn't see your thigh in the curves of the golden calf, or your yearning when you made order manifest in music, or your self-understanding mercy in the wine that let Noah feel the flood drown every inch of his skin, wine that let him escape his patriarchy, that let him be the joyous child your son once was, Lord.

No, they came hurt, afraid, begging for arms to hold them. Your son's followers call themselves his flock. What other god has petted his worshipers as sheep are petted, and loved them for their animal helplessness, their lessness than manhood, their need for a shepherd?

Jesus said he was the son of man. He meant you are a normal god, a daily family god, an unharmful father, an unfrightful brother, yourself somehow a son of woman, a son of a mother. He called you to not forsake him, to walk again in the garden. You wouldn't do that for your son.

It was easier for you to kill him than to grow into his demands on you.

But now the world's reduced for you, isn't it? Here's your church on earth now, two fearful men.

Every day, they try to discover new faces of your face, but they return to each other's eyes.

They ask: If we pray perfectly, if we vanish into you, will we die in the body?

The lust in us, it is not you. Then is it demons? ourselves? Why would you create demons? Why make us mammal?

And what are these women you've created? If we still love lust, can we poison it out of us? Do we drink only the black water, eat only the ugly roots?

If we look at curved roots and see women's legs, shall we leave the dirt on them as we eat? To remind us of what? What is this dirt you have created? Are we dirt? Is dirt demonic?

Living only on dirty roots, our teeth hurt us, our hair falls out, we dream badly. Lo, demons come, dressed as beautiful women.

Why did you ever make anything so beautiful as woman?

What is beauty for? May we ask this without sinning?

May we ask why you do not answer us?

Now we have sinned, in the pride of these questions.

We must destroy even our way of prayer. We must destroy our hearts, our instincts.

We are wrong in everything. Are we even wrong to believe we're wrong?

We're churchmen, gardeners of souls. Who will guide us through the desert of your silence?

You are a loving God. Your love is a black stone we worship, and press our ears to, and wait to hear it speak.

We expound your heart to each other with certainty. We teach our flocks as men who know God.

But in our silence we're tangled liars shrinking from your creation, our hearts shredded, terrified.

Hell will be this church.

So Spek looked out the door into the blue air of the city of flowers.

Because he gazed looking at air and was very still and didn't explain himself, the bishop joined him and gazed as Spek seemed to, into nothing.

They were brethren in accord.

So that when I walked by, both saw me at the same instant. Yet when I looked, I saw them both but felt only Spek.

The bishop hid his eyes, turning away to stare at stone walls, wood floors, at the inner flesh of his eyelids, wishing to annihilate even the image of me.

But Spek, my priest, my messenger, born my husband as I am born his wife, he drank me. He took in all of me at once.

He saw every raindrop that ever fell on my shoulders.

He saw tiny ferocious lights in my eyes, and felt them pierce his flesh.

He saw my forehead cool as agate, and entered it and found himself beyond where wings go, beyond light. He saw my belly framed in wavering tassels, and flickering overtook him. He saw the colors of my skin and they pulled him apart. They dove beneath red, plunging into his belly; they lifted above violet pulling up into his throat. His skin was pulled tight across every color in the sun.

He wanted to marry the mud of earth, to feel my mud belly in his mud hand. Crawling down into the earth was climbing up beyond the world, to the place where need makes the sun combust.

He saw my face see his, he saw me love. Each light within me crackled like a spark across his tongue.

He felt my fingertip unfasten the top of his head. My tongue plunged into the dry powder inside. Boiling wetness was all the order of his thoughts.

Lord, I was easily ready to take him from you. I thanked you Lord, only for keeping him safe and unused in a stone vault until I could find and gather him.

You had your chance, Lord. He tried to love you.

Spek stared into absence after I passed. He tells me the street howled for me *to return. He says the footpath moaned and writhed and cracked.*

This is all from his heart, Lord. You believe I'm only a girl you made and abandoned. You believe you made my dust walk and yawn and eat. But he created me, long before you. His eyes create your creation.

The bishop was standing beside him, eyes shut, swimming against the beauty in his own skin.

Spek looked at him, drugged with wonder. He pronounced me beautiful. The bishop didn't answer, and Spek was alone, he wept and said: Didn't you feel her beauty?

The bishop said: You mean to say, God's beauty in her.

Spek said fervently: God's beauty at least. Every bit of it in her.

The other said: God will judge her.

Spek said: God will envy her.

The other said: I see the parable in your heart. Here is a harlot, who works hard to paint herself to enmesh her lovers. She dresses to keep her lovers enslaved to her mystery. Do we sinners work as hard to beautify our souls for God? No—we lack faith in our soul's beauty, and compound all our sins with sloth.

Spek was silent.

Yes, *said the bishop,* yes yes that is the parable. We must be ready for our bridegroom.

But the bishop stood unready, anxious, judging Spek, afraid to judge him.

Spek was under a different sky. He breathed honey, he swam the river of honey.

His mind was a palm, cupping my sex. His heart was soaked in every sweet spice.

The bishop told him: That whore will lose her beauty one day. She's a hag, if you can see.

He answered: She is all of beauty. *And he turned his face to the wall, and wept.*

Bishop said: She'll die, God will destroy her.

In tears Spek answered: She'll drown God in beauty. God, why have you drowned yourself?

Bishop shouted: You are standing in Hell.

He answered: Don't pray for me. God gave you a world. He flings beauty into your arms. He's not tempting you, why would he do that? Beauty is his pulse. He's showing himself to you. He's the bridegroom, sleep with him!

Bishop said: She's not from God, she's a demon from Hell.

He answered: Who made demons? Are the flowers demons? Is your beautiful voice a demon, brother? Are your deep eyes a demon? Don't you know you're beautiful? Look how the knot in your heart shows itself so clearly. God gave you a clear face so lovers could see you suffer, and come soothe you. That's why your pain's not secret. So we can touch each other's hearts.

Bishop said: A demon has entered you, I will remove it.

He answered: Don't. Don't touch the center of me, where this sweetness lives. Don't tell me your judgment. Don't say words like demon, don't blaspheme.

The demon is time. The hour after I lie down, before I fall asleep, that is the demon God sends. My dreams are demons. Desolation.

Live in dryness then, live in waiting, live in anger, live in the God who hates the beauty he makes. Help the bridegroom cut his arms off, cut his head off, cut his sex off. Hand him the blade and receive his praise, let that be your joy.

But do not touch me.

While he said this to his brother, Lord, I was lying face down on the footpath, sobbing too hard to breathe.

People of the city went and told Spek I was there, so that he walked out of his church and came to me.

He knelt beside me, so close to me. His body was free of its shell. But he wasn't mine, he would have to return to that church, always, he was married there. I must not love this man.

I told him: Your god, he forbids you to love. He must be more powerful than any god. Does he have your face, husband? Is he like you? The cause? Then let your god own my soul. I accept him—please teach me to pray the way you do.

My beloved replied: How can he hear us pray? He's breathless, adoring you.

He said: What have you done with God's universe? You've put it into the curve of your neck, it hovers there.

(*You don't understand. I'm a woman who loves many men.*)

God is said to be like you. He's said to give and give, and to ask only that we serve him in his beauty.

(*I know my sins. They're uncountable. Now I make you break your vow.*)

Your eyes have forgiven you. Your eyes teach me enough to forgive you myself.

Wife. Miracle.

You walked past me, alone, and I forgot the hierarchy of truths.

All the creation hangs on your wrist.

Where the air touches your wrist is a sacred place.

You paint the air with gold, you thread a gold hair through my body.

Now your wrist travels down my body, up my breath, each time you move.

If I breathe in, I feel your face against my chest. If I breathe out, I feel my belly against your back.

You're the vapor God forgot how to breathe, you're the vision his worshippers lost in the dark. You're the heat I tried to live without, you're the purpose.

You took the world away, you took God away. You are a whole world resting on top of me. Your beauty is geography, your eyes are philosophy, your breath is the sun.

Just imagine, the bishop expected me to speak to him, after I'd stared at you with worship rushing through my body.

To speak to him as he averted his eyes from you, trying to hate you.

When I woke to the world, through the gold light of you, I barely saw this bishop looking at my face.

The empty part of him he calls by his own name, this part is shocked and frightened.

He believes he sees a demon in my eyes. I forgive him.

The full part of him that's nameless, that part knows your beauty.

That part knows you are the whole world.

That you're the light of the heart, that you're the holy spirit, that you're the love we talk about constantly.

Why are you crying? You never have to cry.

(*Exorcise the demon from me.*)

I wouldn't change you. Your demon is holy.

(*If you won't baptize me, I'll kill myself. As a dead woman I'll pry open heaven and tell our god your sin.*)

God isn't powerful enough to look into your eyes.

(*What are you saying? I don't want to destroy your soul.*)

Where did you learn about souls, and God, and demons?

(*I've slept with Christians, and heard them shout prayers as they came, and darker prayers afterwards. There was one beautiful man I baptized, using honey and* earth. I painted the cross and the fish on his belly. I have heard that Jesus believed in love.)

I'm his feet, you are his wound.

(Don't look at me. Cast the beauty out of me. I want to eat the stones of the desert.)

Why?

(Because your eyes tell me about perfection. Now I want to bathe in the purity of your eyes. Remember your holy vow, that's the beauty in you. I love you. I'm not going to be the one who destroys your sixteen years of beautiful denial.)

My husband closed his eyes and said: God and I live in darkness. He's given me only his name to live on. In return for his name, I promised him my life. Is that fair?

(He is a god, I know, but I don't know his name. Is it a mystery?)

His name is God. I said it a thousand times a day, I lived on the sound of it.

(Please drown me in your god. Shred my sins. Destroy me in you so I can 't ruin you.)

I gave my vow to God, I married him in this flesh.

(Yes yes, then baptize me too. Pour his name over me, I'll be your sister.)

You'll be my sister. But my mind will rest on your belly, and rise and fall gently.

(We'll be free of the flesh. I'll have no belly or breath.)

You'll be my sister, my eyes will weep the honey on your tongue.

(Don't you believe in your god? Don't you love him beyond sunlight? Didn't he create your eyes? I love him for your eyes. I won't ever hurt your marriage with him. Just pray. Tell him you've captured an enemy. Offer to burn me in his nostrils.)

Why did I see you. Why does God send me angels.

(No no no no no. Speak your heart to him. You are his. Your pale heart is more beautiful than a million of my mocha-skinned bodies. Let him fall in love with you again. Let him hold you, let him whisper in your hair, let him heat you between his palms.)

He's not that kind of god.

(He must be. He created you, he married you, he preserved you for me in this bubble. He must have your eyebrows, your gentle voice. He must be a god of honeysuckle, he must exist to forgive, he must be the god of embracing.)

I've spent sixteen years with him and I can tell you. He is an embrace of stone.

(He created the world. He made rain run down the stalk of the lily. He created the soul of water. He put the rivers in us that want to merge.)

He did, but I've never seen him cry. When I cry, he recedes. Maybe he cries for himself in the dark. He knows very well there is waste after all this, like there was void before. We who praise him, we die out of his creation. This is his love for the world.

(A moment of love lasts longer than the void. If you know that, he'll know it too.)

He doesn't seem to feel me.

(He's your left hand, as it remembers the feeling of holding a chrysalis without crushing it.)

No; my hand is dreaming your hair.

(Pray to your god in your hand's dreams. We'll recover ourselves for his sake. If I destroy your faith I can't allow myself to exist.)

You're the plane of heaven. Your shoulders are stronger than God. I love you more than light. You've taken me over.

(Call that God in me. You're feeling him but you don't realize. Pray to him in my hair.

If I hold your hair in my hand, my religion will turn to sweet smoke in my mouth. How can I not inhale?

(*God created sweetness and smoke and the taste of my skin and the name for honey.*)

The god my father doesn't live in this city of flowers. If you mean this, if you truly want to see him, he lives where the void shows through. We have to go to the desert.

(*He's the sky over silence. That silence in your face. Good, we'll go together. I'll be a cactus in the desert, a stone, three stones.*)

If you follow me, I'll follow you. I want to give you anything you ask. You want to be baptized and purified of your flesh?

(*Purified of sin. I see sin in your eyes when you talk about your god. You don't love him at all.*)

...no.

(*He's not your god then. What do you love?*)

I love your power that's holding me suspended between the earth and the sky.

I love the small cathedral of your voice, your body-church with drum-skin walls, with resonant doors, all the shapes of you sounding in your speech.

I love the new skin of you in the sunlight. I love the pain I feel with my eyes closed against you.

You've been inside me ten thousand years. I love my flesh's memory of you.

I love the brutal power of the earth in you, that grips me and slams me against your body, and insists we love, insists that I live in torment till I can grip you to me, insists that I writhe with the need to touch the center of your body and make new children out of us.

I love that pain has vanished in you, that death has stopped, time has stopped. I love not being here, but being in you.

I love the sky when you look at it, and the faces of fishmongers when they please you, and God when he seems beautiful to you.

But I'm married to this god. And he isn't in you. He's not found in ephemeral things, he's only in the eternal. Stones broken by the sun, teeth of sharks petrified in the mountain. He's in long slow processes that harden and darken. He smites so there will be less moisture in his sopping creation. He rages against the honey of your sex. He created every drop, so I don't understand why.

Let's go to the desert to ask him. Let's pray.

(But we can't touch. You have to be faithful to your god, for as long as you can understand him. You begin the prayer, as we walk. Begin now, my love.)

I have to pray to him through you. I have to remake the trinity from nothing.

Wife. He is there in you. Each inch of your infinite height has been the goal of my life, your complex eternal flesh that's new every dawn, your flesh that's washed in new rain every moment, your flesh that has meaning connected to it like nerves. To touch you makes *meaning* feel my touch, *meaning* turns over and sighs for my hand.

Your eyebrows say: reach into me and dissolve my pain. I'll never reach far enough into you.

The belly of you is a moonscape, I can't be Spek here, I can't hear language here. I worship the substance that takes away words. Now that I've touched you, I'll crush the chain of being to keep my fingers here. I'll unravel heaven to live in your breath.

For this flesh here, for this infinite land of flesh, for this I'll give all of time, past and future.

Into this tiny spiral of flesh, into this heat I cup in my hand, into this surface and depth pour every thought I've ever had, every breath of my wishes, every preference, every memory, every vision.

With the soles of your feet, the whirlpool of your hair, creature of joints and muscles, animal smaller than I am, with the front of you and back of you, your inside and outside, the surface of your eyelids and the depths of your eyes, I'll annihilate all the world, I'll annihilate all my past and the past of every creature, I'll annihilate the basis.

For an infinite minute I aim myself directly at God, I steal a piece of God's own flesh to eat, I melt into him to become him. And there's a landscape of you. God is noplace here. I hunt him down through every inch of your flesh, till only your eyebrows still draw me in, eyebrows still in anguish, showing the pain I haven't soothed, still showing the lack in me. Your eyebrows are where God is, and God's begging me, keep trying, please save me, I'll forgive you if only you can be greater, still greater, still greater.

When you sleep, your eyebrows are smooth, God's forgotten us. The plain of your body is the real earth, my arms are sky holding you. This is our creation.

What is the Trinity?

The Trinity is the Three. First, God. God is God, incomprehensible. All, nothing.

Christ is the loyal wife whose husbands all leave her, who frets at her failures, who dances the dance of "dancing badly" and drapes the sky in black, forgiving men their explosive refusal to die.

The Holy Spirit is the husband who yearns infinitely for what he can't see, wraps his body around the whole earth looking for the hidden core within some unmet woman who will finally be truth and joy and completion.

But greater than the Trinity is the woman who destroys men with her presence, who's the spiral in the dream of every heart. She's greater than God. She's the heat in creation, she's God's helpless need to create. She's the yes

God speaks while trying to say no. In her, only in her, he adores himself. She scatters her face among the nations, to bring about drama, to tangle emotions, to cause more sagas, more songs, more sculptures, more pain and uprooting. She's the tree that grows through stone.

With her, God punished himself. He let her take the quiet church and ring it like a bell. He touched her hand and she unbalanced the placid continents so they tipped up into mountains, so there'd be avalanches, also cliffs for suicide, hiding-caves, black hidden valleys. Then, even as he forbade her, she took the creation out of his hands and ripped it in two parts, and made the parts desire each other, she made them fight, she made them need.

And God, who refused to learn from her, ripped me into two persons, then forbade those persons to embrace. Because when those persons touch, there is eternal love. God the father, the one who remembered eternity before our universe, he couldn't bear an eternity of Eden. He had to return to nothingness. It's what he knows.

Look at his sky. He gave his whole creation to vacuum, stone and fire. Earth is just a chip of green. The night sky was his heart.

Wife, creator. In your world a man can dissolve his religion. Here I can change.

In your sunlight, men in the city of flowers who stay with their wives feel themselves dying. They're loyal, dogged, flesh half-stone. They watch the sun wanting to dive into it and immolate their pain.

Wife, creator, you made mating into time. You tore the day so half would be night. On the first of your nights the husbands in the city of flowers grew desperate.

That first night, you dropped the sun and it died. It never reassured the earth, never softly explained "I'll be back soon, I'm on a voyage to the world you don't see, to the place you've never been, but I'll shine on no other world till I return to you." No, the sun left us. Husbands walked away from their wives that night. I left my Christ alone in his stone tomb. Your incomprehensible moon, your moon that changes objects into their opposite, that glows and remains cold, your moon rose and beautified all faces by hiding them. It made every form desirable and dim, soft, unreachable, light even yearning out of stone. I merged with that night and I never loved my Lord again.

Now every night in the city, husbands float free. Girls wearing bangles and toe-rings, nose-rings and anklets, they light moon-lanterns, they walk through the streets to the homes of their lovers and wait outside the door, shining. Inside are angry voices, arguing, sobbing. Then her lover appears, trying to abolish anger from his face, trying to look fun, fun-loving, fun-having. Behind him is a wife's muffled weeping. But he's looking through the lantern halo of his new girl, he's gazing at her face lit by the lantern on her left cheek and by the blue moon on her right cheek. The weeping of his wife, that's not fun, that's not beautiful, that's not glowing with two lights. He wants to believe in what the moon shows him, so he believes. He doesn't want to remember his wife, so he forgets her.

His new girl, she doesn't want to hear weeping, only laughing, so she laughs. She believes she's different from a wife, she could never be a dull woman trapped inside a house: because of the moon, because of bangles and anklets, because the sun is gone and a mist of your Holy Spirit is everywhere.

Across the city of flowers, wives mourn, their beautiful eyes wept out with anger. They curse love, curse their marriage, they curse themselves for discovering and creating and believing in such a husband. They curse the nighttime that never existed in their youth, but now makes new girls beautiful. They curse time that's so long, and distance that's so far, and their flesh that's in such pain. They open their jewel-boxes to throw bangles and anklets out the window, shouting about trash and deception and betrayal. They take the best linen shirt of their husband, and lay it out on the ground in the inner garden, and stab it through the belly with the knife that's used to end the lives of animals, the knife that makes lambs and goats die, the knife that destroys the soft eyes that look at you and trust you, that come to you and nuzzle you, that make you laugh, eyes you love, eyes that must die so that we can live in the sunlight, so that we can eat, so that we will not stay hungry forever. And in the moon the stabbed shirt floats on the ground, it seems to rise, it seems free to go anyplace it wants, to wrap its arms around any girl's dress. It's a piece of the moon and a knife can't pin it to the earth, the earth has no strength now, the earth is weeping for the sun.

Thousands of men betray their wives on this night, and all across the city wives lie alone in their beds, calling on the moon to shatter and fall out of the sky.

Lord Jesus, was I the bridegroom? I lay in bed alone. There in your temple I felt your absence terribly. It wasn't girls of flowers on the street I wanted, plaited hair without meaning. But it wasn't your hair either, Jesus, pickled with meaning. It wasn't hips of skinny girls without redemption, hips like drinks of alcohol. Nor your starved hips, revealed as a gory bed of suffering. Yours is a heaven where there's nobody to marry. A place where we praise God and not our beloveds. And God sits, without a wife, hearing our praise maybe, never replying.

Lord Jesus, if I love red, her skin turns red. If orange, her eyes turn orange. If I love basil, her shoulders smell like that. If I love salmon, her tongue tastes like that. I won't be surprised except with joy. I won't be confused or unsure. What I dreamed is on the table for me, in my eyes she reads what I dream and in her body she dances it back to me.

She's false, if the sunset is false. She's false, if the stars are false. No, the sunset's not performed only for me. No, the stars aren't mine to pluck down and take home. I'm here, Lord. In your house, not in her arms. I could still awaken, I could still refuse. I could stay here and live without solace, I could ignore the free gift. This soft fragment of sun could be left behind on the footpath, her body-brewed liquor of moon I could spit into the fire.

Instead I'd live here loyally, without joy, without solace, without feeling the heat of meaning. Unkissed, I'd wait for truth to love me. Truth will usually tell you what is not: You are not loveable, love is nothing, nobody is loveable, love is lying flattery, you will die alone, death is truth, nothing is anything, everything is nothing, praise his name.

My Christ, I'd end by believing in your father's laws. Since nothingness is a law, since death is justice, I'd worship the God who punishes, I'd praise him. He's not a girl for me to adore, he's a man and I don't love him. Bitter, I'd ask him to punish the wrongdoers—I, the righteous man, would rat out all the wrongdoers. Our Father would then punish the wrongdoers, and I'd feel praised! I'd feel warm!

A wife, singing only for me, looking into my eyes to see who I am, to see what I feel, she could have given me warmth. There would have been no punishment, only reward. There would have been no judgment by a stone god, only beauty's soft hand on my forehead, love's gentle hand on my back.

I am married to Christ, yet I prefer a dancing goddess, I am a wrongdoer.

And this immense catastrophe comes from whoever created the heat, and the empty space that needs heat. Whoever gave sight to the eye of my wife, so she can see into my eyes and know what God's withheld from me.

In my heart she closes her eyes and opens them, because when we sleep together her eyes will close and open.

I see her toss her hair, because when we sleep together, her hair will be tangled.

She lolls her head, because when we sleep together our heads will rest on feathers.

In this night, as I lay in Christ's bed, somewhere my wife washes her hair in cloves and vanilla, she paints her toenails with red cotton paste, she adorns herself with bangles and a thigh-clasp of silver and anklets of black coral. I scent, I see. It's the day of darkness, the moon's swallowed the flesh of the sun.

Beside the seashore we walk on sand and flowers.

She sings the song about the sultan who destroyed the treasure by digging for it.

The song about the sun that wilts the flower as it gives blush to it.

The song about moonlight the color of the land of the dead.

She sings about the sea that grips secrets between its legs, the black sea that conceals everything there is, that only speaks to say Nobody knows me, nobody knows me.

The song about the ocean of vicious currents, the ocean made of individual drops of water, where we can't live, where we go to drown.

The permanent ocean that won't move aside for us, the permanent ocean we can't drink up, that holds and floats and softens us, that finally disassembles us. That song.

The beach I dream in my stone bed is decorated like an infinite stage, pillars stand by the sea wrapped in garlands, hung with flowers. Flowers are scattered on the waves. Drummers play, the yazh and flute play, and my wife of slender waist, she of long neck, she can sing me songs that fit the harmonies of all the other music we hear as we walk along. She can suit her song perfectly to all other songs, even as she sings only to me.

She gives her eyes to me like a river giving water, never slowing, never pausing, never stinting, never distracted, never in fear of running out of her substance, never protecting herself, never showing doubt in her curved eyebrows.

She's God, of whom she's barely heard. She's God instead of God, who failed to show himself to me from one decade to the next, she shows herself. She's God instead of God, who stayed in the sky and never spoke, she whispers continuously. She's God who can't possibly exist, she palpably surrounds me. God, he drugged with praise who curses with silence, she sings right into my ear.

We're walking the beach. She's asking me for things:

Oh man with a name, let me take your name inside my mouth. Let me say Spek, Spek.

Oh man with a mouth, take my name into your mouth, let me hear Qurratulain.

Spek, Spek, creature of sunlight, tell me if you've seen my future life.

I know all fears, I who am full of fear. I know your fears.
But step off the cliff. It's certain death. Step off the cliff into the palm of my hand. I won't treat you badly. Don't fear I'll ask you for bangles or jewels. I won't ask for clothing or for anything you can touch with a finger. I won't ask you for a wedding ring, Spek, Spek.

Just tell me, among the waves of your hair, is there a message for me? In the web of your nerves, do you feel my passage? Am I traveling upward or am I falling?

Your eyes that searched for love in the twelve directions, your eyes that now only look at my eyes—do they know how our life ends?

When you were taken down out of the bright air, when you were created, when you were forged with weightless tools, when you were born into sunlight, when you first tasted the water of earth, wasn't I in the taste? Didn't you see me in the motion of the earth? Don't I belong here, or am I lost on beautiful earth by mistake?

The sea makes me worship. The strewn flowers are my skin washing over the world.

Did I commit a crime, to need you this way? Does moonlight make more mistakes than the sun? Does it create women who have noplace to rest, women like birds that fly and never alight, women who love even the air and will kiss a green wall for its color and cry?

Beautiful wife, in your yearning, in the suffering of your brow, in the quiver of your mouth, in the many signs of your devoted pain, you're wounded in me.

When you kiss me, you're turning our souls on a wheel. When you ask my advice, you're circling around yourself, you're capturing yourself. When you wait for me to speak, and empty your mind to receive my words, you're a hawk who waits on the pillar to be shot, and watches the bowman draw back his bow, and waits for the arrow as if death were beauty. This is the simple path, the single path hemmed-in by vines and flowers, bordered by walls of flesh and light, no detour or destination—the circular infinite path that only waits, that never moves off its own path, the path of itself. I love the silence of your unmoving eyes that spiral in. You set the goal in front of my feet, and take my hand, and lead me to take one step, and I step against your body, I reach your easy goal.

When you sing for my ears, you're a deer who comes out of the woods and finds the salt lick, and gives up her grace and speed for that taste. She's very quiet, she tastes the salt, and quivers as her body still remembers the open forest behind her.

I've visited your skin, I've tasted your nerves, I've sung into your eyes and ears and belly, I've watched your soul at the moment your name left you, when you forgot me and became your whole creation.

Within you are unvisited gardens, innumerable scents and radiances, the thoughts contained in all libraries, every song echoing, every word singing, every syllable speaking, the light of every sun since the beginning, and 72,000,000 open passageways you freely travel.

You and I are your own creation, you create us every instant and we wait for you. We're there in your eyes and I see us, we're in the skin of your lips, under your fingernails, we're there in the arches of your feet, the sudden scoop of your hands, the flicker of your mouth. The light of your eyes, the light of your eyes.

I have a sweet mouth from the touch of your mouth, and sweet ears from the sound of your song, and listen, wife, do you hear that? Do you hear? I couldn't pray to him, and now Christ is leaving me, my Christ is walking away, the golden one is walking, leaving the city ahead of us, entering the desert before us, wandering into the waste.

Is my Christ walking, is the silver one walking, is he bitter at losing me? Is he crossing the desert to a land where God is unknown, where pain doesn't rule hearts, where no father will command him to pour out his love?

Can he find the sweeter land where God's finger doesn't reach, where hearts aren't compelled, where no one lies awake listening to the whisper in the absence?

Can he find the land of peace where the house is built for shelter and beauty and not for the salvation of the builder? Can he find the land where flowers are loved and never picked for offerings?

Has he walked far away from God, has he walked into the place where the wood-carver carves what the wood asks for? Where the baker only listens to what the yeast says? Where no one suffers waiting for his reward, for his result, for the pay, for the judgment?

Because he has no enemy, God is his enemy.

Wife, angel, woman, if I tell you about your shining spiraling hair, you say, who are you talking about?

If I tell you my bishop has wounded my heart, you say, who is he? And you show a bishop to me inside-out.

The eyes my bishop stares at me, inside-out these are a night sky that looks at itself.

The words my bishop uses to circumscribe me, inside-out these are the music every creature makes in its head, in silence.

Wife. Outside our home I'll tie a rope from a tree to the base of a mushroom, so the tree won't run away.

Wife, in our house there'll be noplace to serve guests, instead a fishnet in the corner, bundled and tied tight so it can't snare anybody.

We'll walk the world free as swans who don't care what crows say. As swans we'll sit at the foot of the world and see beauty everyplace.

You show me beauty in the faces that pass, when I wasn't looking at the faces.

You see the beauty of the flower withering and petals scattering.

Every day the sun makes your skin shimmer and your face glow. Every night you gasp when you see the moon, never losing pleasure in it.

Moon, you see what my wife is to me. So weep, moon, let your arms grow weak, let your legs give out, fall to the sand. Cry salt for the sea to swallow. That's the droplet in the sea. Weep blood for the gulls to steal. Cry into the eyes of laughing men who laugh at you weeping. If you don't weep now, then when you return to your sun you will find it missing, you'll see endless time where its promise was, and you'll weep. That's the sea in a droplet.

Qurratulain you know my name, say the name. Let the name crunch on your tongue, *Spek*, let the name whistle in your lips, *Spek*. All I ask is to hear my name touch your mouth.

There, I spoke your name. The vapors of your name, the perfume of your name, the flesh of your name, start to yearn in my mouth, but this is disaster. Your name translates you into the world's names for you: homewrecker, sinner. If you're a sinner, I have to flee you and follow my Lord where he goes; my life is his despite his invisible face. So with your name on my tongue, I breathe it out, I blow it away, I put it on the wind, I send it to the ocean, I send it to the sky, I don't speak it again, but now under the sun it's the Lord's day, the day of ordinary time, of irritated voices, of flowers gasping for air, flowers cut from their roots, flowers brown, flowers grey.

God takes desire out of us, he pushes a wind across the face of the sea and rips lovewords out of our mouths, bleaches color from the mourning flowers, wipes music from the hearts of weary musicians, scrubs perfume from the lovely bodies, and he blows all these treasures of scent and song and breathless whispers across the city and beyond the desert.

In all the houses of the city, abandoned wives awaken when they scent that wind at the windows, their eyes open and in a few seconds pain remembers to find them, they're alone.

On the beach, thousands of husbands argue with their mistresses. They scowl at the faces they have kissed, the skin of those faces repels them now, so that they sing these stanzas:

"A new goddess has come out of the sea, she has come disguised as a girl with eyes like blood-stained spears, she is the god of death.

"The strength of my body is lost in the crashing of waves that sound like war-machines, the sense of my words is lost in the wind that sounds like the shrieking of widows.

"My serene life is in turmoil, it is this girl's fault, she did this to me, I'm not to blame. My kind and soulful wife is wounded, it's not my fault, it's the fault of the almond-eyed one.

"When she looked at me with open eyes, she was using guile. When she looked at me trustingly, that was her snare. When she complimented me, she knew I can't resist a kind word.

"She doesn't know I'm married, that's because she doesn't want to know. She who knows every desire of my heart, who sees my weakness for her, she should have protected my wife, she should have known I'm married.

"It's the fault of the moon, it's the fault of the swelling sea, it's the fault of the honey-filled lily, it's the fault of the cool grove where we walked, the destroying beauty of her face, her face.

"When her face promised me perfect happiness, it lied to me. When her face told me about a land where everyone possesses everything he desires, that was a lie. She is love, deceitful beyond measure.

"At the lake I drew a picture of the swan we saw and I handed it to her. She sat against a juniper and propped the picture on her thighs and gave her eyes to it, she let it sing to her eyes, she loved it with her open heart and wore it out with loving. What did she love in the picture? How did I draw such a picture?

"I stepped into a whirlwind and lost the things I knew. Even as a child I knew where to find down and where to find up. I knew that whirlwinds come from the sky and clouds. Whirlwinds don't come from myself, whirlwinds don't come from a girl's face, or her hips, or her feet, or the silver ring around her toe. I used to know that, as a child I knew it."

Eternal wife, Qurratulain: all night while I was with you, my Christ lay in the desert alone. He heard music coming from the seashore. He smelled the flowers of the ceremony. He smelled the spices of the delicacies being cooked in the pits all along the sand. But he ate no meal, he waited for my return. He ate no bread, waiting for my footstep. He drank no sparkling drink, no sweetened milk, no still water. He held nothing in his hands, he took nothing for himself.

Now I must go meet the anger of my Christ, now I must see the tears of my Lord. My morning has been heartbreaking, my afternoon has been desperate beauty, my evening will be grief and woe.

Yes come with me to the desert, slim-waisted girl. Come tell my Christ you're to blame for my waywardness. If he looks in your eyes he'll believe you. I always believe when I look in your eyes.

Up the sandy hill the beach touches the road, and there the vendors are ready. They are selling items for husbands to appease wives. Shall I buy these for my Lord?

Here are blue pots of salve for a wife's angry eyes—

a purple veil to hide her grief—

here are pearls and coral and lapis in gifting boxes—

and flowers carved from jade, flowers carved from faience, flowers that will last forever, faithful flowers—

here's even a crowd of men who will rent themselves to you as houseguests. Take one home and your wife will have to feed him, entertain him, she will not be able to shout at you as long as he is there—

I'll bring you to the desert, little wife. Christ can't be angry when he sees you. Here is a priest sitting in a glass box who knows the hearts of women, he can sell us a lie to tell the Lord, a lie he'll want to believe, a lie to tempt him, to make him love even you.

But I love being with you. So we linger in the stalls among distressed, hungover husbands, and I look at the trinkets as if choosing the best among them. We smile at the rental houseguests, who're now laughing and playing cards and gossiping about clients they've seen today.

We embrace in front of the wise man in the glass box, the seller of lies, the priest of both Hermes and Thoth with the fire of confusion in his tongue, whose thoughts are mercury, who can appear and vanish again, who makes words stay together in stanzas, words that should never be able to touch each other. The priest who creates lies like prayer, who makes beauty usable, makes stories that never took place become true. Who will make a small lie for a coin, and for a huge bag of coins will build a lie as powerful as a god.

He sees the past and future, but only as stuff for weaving. He can declare an apple holy and it changes, it becomes holy. He can declare the same apple evil if required. The apple suffers, but he's unhurt by its suffering.

He turns one house into three large houses, he turns seven women into none. He nullifies any promise, and causes faith and love to be lost in memory, lost in a noise of laughter. He easily turns a five-year marriage into a mere interlude, a small incident, and will make a sixteen-year marriage even nothing if you pay him well.

He'll never do work others can do for him. If a woman cries out "Maybe I wasn't good enough to my husband," he only nods. If she will abase herself, and make white into black, and crawl on the ground, the priest will say to the husband, "Your payment to me brought this about."

Alms to him will increase the softness under your feet. Alms will make this world misty and dim, and cause the bright world to become one opinion among many. He turns the city of flowers into a floating island with no exact shape. He makes the sun into a stone that gives no light. He puts a second moon in the sky so day's like night, uncertain and shifting.

Without a coin, he sits very still, without a silver coin his body has no animal joy, without a gold coin, his mind can't lie.

I speak to him without a coin, without good metal. Teach us to pray, I say.

"No," he sings, "give a coin, a coin."

He looks at us and knows we don't have money, then he knows we don't need any.

He wants to sit silently, but even without pay his body makes him restless to damage things. He hasn't conquered his body, not in fifty years of sitting in a glass box.

"If you would pay me you'd hear a story that would save you, a story you could use.

"You want to know how to seduce God. It's too late for both of you.

"You give nothing. So you'll hear the worthless unimproved story. The godless, with no money, they hear only truth. That's what makes them bitter."

"Don't torture a friend of Thoth, thief. Steal a coin and give it, I'll show you how to go back to your god. I'll give you double sight, thief. Your god will love you again, this dancing girl's face will be his shrine. When you're in bed and holding her, your god will be tricked, he'll think you're worshipping creation. One gold coin and one silver coin."

Quarratulain, you asked the priest softly: *Tell us the source of pain. Tell us the error of our lives that chained my husband to an absent god. Then show us the new path.*

Priest turned his face away. Who will withstand the heart of my wife? Who will not be annihilated at the hush of her face? Her liquid voice makes this world flow.

He didn't speak after that for years, and in his glass box the rays of the sun wouldn't touch him.

Wife, Qurratulain, come to the desert, I'll marry you. I'll give up my arms and legs, and face and hands, and enter you and never leave. My belly won't have to yearn for yours, it will be yours. Under the sky of your mind I'll wander free of God.

Every loaf of bread I've eaten without you is a lodestone that pulls me to you. Every cup of water I've poured for myself is a wave that presses toward you. And I'll taste your mouth forever, like drinking all of a river.

God in me tries to make me imagine losing you. But the paths away from you all are tangled and I confess I love your face and hips and crave all your bright body. Isn't this God?

So let's escape this city of dancers and flowers and lazing women and men seeking fame and the judgment in every eye.

Let God be darkness and let us hide there.

Let's return to the womb where we were born together, the dark place outside time.

We'll hold Jesus, we'll explain to him, we'll help him, we'll create him. Or if he won't listen to us, then we'll hammer his head and pull out his bones to prevent him creating any more eternal pain, eternal anger, eternal unkindness. And I'll awaken in your arms, purity with the rounded form.

Together we'll subtract God from time, and live in the kiss. You breathing in my heart, me breathing in your heart.

Eternal fool that I am, everything I say is foolish, my wife has to tell me words that you say to a goat. My wife has to explain this world to me, gently, so I don't feel my idiocy.

Now she says: *You have to go to the desert. I believe you. But you have to learn.*

She says: *I'll go with you. I'll love you there. I'll brighten the brightness for you, I'll clear the clarity for you. If I ever hurt you, I'll walk off into the sun and melt there like sand. If I ever hurt you, I'll cross the desert and empty myself into the river, and flow into the sea. But I'll never hurt you, I'll be your own wishes. I'll breathe like your soul breathes, you'll feel me under you as you walk, softening your footfalls. You'll feel me in your legs, pacing, climbing for you. I'll be sunlight at night, moonlight in the day.*

And in your homeless desert, I'll be foundation, timbers, a protecting roof, quieting walls, soft light in the window, and the color in every color. You won't see me, you'll see the wind. You won't hear me, you'll hear an ocean. Waves whispering my gratitude to you.

God, this is how she talks to me. And how do you talk to me?

In his thirtieth year your son's vision came to him. He spoke miracles, but he spoke in pain. Him too, did you drive him out of his skin?

But yours is the Creation. Yours. I pledged my soul to you forever.

So take us both, so we understand. Turn her into the dust of your feet. Turn my memory of her eyes into the black ash of your night sky.

I'll prepare to be bridegroom. For the sake of your undulating wasteland, your naked tan sand-drifts, I'll abandon the belly of my infinite wife. I'll prepare my wasting virgin body for its only death.

I've bathed in my last stream, and applied a violet ointment I've never known, and combed my hair for the last time. I misshaped my hair into a halo of golden flax for you, a huckster's boast, a promise.

Onto my shining body I've put a fresh linen shirt and a pair of wedding trousers. Here's my face, bright with the darkness of this vision.

I'm dressing for you, Lord, today you take my body. I'll walk onto your shoulder and melt there.

The pockets of these ritual trousers contain nothing but silence.

Our church has a kitchen, many kinds of food are here. But to eat from the House of the Lord would be eating the vision. I won't let this body eat the beauty it's desperate for. I won't feed this body anything but your name.

Let this church be. The walls are your stones, they'll know what to do next. Let its door be an open mouth, to be fed with the bodies of thieves or the souls of the unwary. I'll never see this place again. I love you, Lord, save me, destroy me.

I don't possess her. She's yours, alongside me. She is your air, Lord.

Here's where Christ walked out of my life, the place in the road where the city of flowers gives up its body. At the western edge of my city, where it falls off into desert, here our language is eaten by snakes. Here the city collapses, exhausted, sick of itself, sick of its belief in wine, sick of the recooked joys of beauty, on its knees weeping over the continual setting of the sun, weeping over the deaths of every person who ever lived, already weeping over the deaths of those to be born. At this place beyond the broken outer path, the city bleeds its body into the desert. It says "My idea goes no further," "This has all been circling," "I loved the flicker of a smile on a woman's face as she walked through my streets entangled in her unknowable thoughts, and that flicker was brief, it didn't return, it can't be kissed and held, it's gone, gone."

Right here, your desert pushes sand back against the mud and clay and says nothing, says *nothing* loudly *nothing*, says *waste*, says *here it is*, says *this is what it is*. This is the border of you, Lord. I give myself to you. Take. The emptiness of your sky demands not to be filled. The dot of me won't fill your sky even a dot's worth.

My wife is standing beside me. I hear her breathing. She's the size of your earth, her breath is deeper than any emptiness. I hear her breathing. She's greater than all your suns.

Her breath is beauty, marriage, devotion, longing, destruction. One breath of hers is bigger than this sky.

A girl of the earth, created by the earth, creator of the earth. She sits in the mud here at the edge of our city and paints her face with mud. She divides her body with a single line of mud, forehead to sex, and the line is the word for birdflight. She drives her fingers into the clay here at the last few steps before the waste begins, and smears clay onto the front of my shining linen shirt, and I close my eyes, unable to breathe a prayer. I feel her open this shirt and smear my chest with weeping clay. Wet clay fills every corner of the sky with the hum of her sourceless light. It even reaches my infinitely empty heart, and fills it to bursting.

All my life, the front of my chest was a vacuum where the light of gods never reached. My wife of clay hands is only the small size of her body, she only exists here. I open my eyes, clutch her body in both my hands and tell her, the size of you is small, you're very small.

She's filled this vacancy forever with her small breath. She's the size of a yes my Lord could never speak. "Beloved, true wife, say to me what you want to say. Anything. I'll say yes. I'll turn from God for you."

She says nothing, but weeps and hugs the earth behind me, weeps into the earth. She shakes her head and her hair flops in the dust. She doesn't delete my Lord with a gesture, she loves my love for him. Yet he calls her a great sin.

I married the Lord, and not my true wife.

She covers herself with dust. She's become the dust. God has nothing to fear from her. She's my past, though I'd never met her. The clay on my wedding clothes, God created. God's shirt is still shining, his body is clean, he's pure of desires and without fault. The blank spot in front of my chest is invisible, I myself can't see it, what I feel is normal, everybody has a blank spot there. And God will marry me because he forgives my blank spot, because he can't see its infinity, because he's so busy hearing prayers and withholding his blessings.

So that I am a brother of the desert from this moment. One who eats prayer and becomes light, alone.

I stepped onto the cracked place, I set my foot onto the wound in the earth. Even wounded the earth holds me up. Here is the flesh of my marriage to death.

I've told her no. I spoke to her like a fool about the beauty of purity, and of the bubble of peace that would softly burst one day and gently kill me. I've said no, I've told her to go pray for her soul, I've told her to find Jesus. Jesus has broken loose in my chest and jagged pieces of him travel through my blood, the pain is terrible.

I've run away to the desert, the city of flowers is behind me. There's no path here, yet she's followed.

Her power over men, the beauty that made men gaze and dream, it doesn't apply to the desert. Here she doesn't tense against her desirability, she doesn't feed others her beauty, she doesn't keep it by disguising it, she doesn't keep it by hating it. She doesn't hold on to beauty and she doesn't drop it on the ground. Instead she has power over power. In the city of flowers she wasn't just a flower; in the desert she's not a desert snake who is stalked and trapped, dug out and killed, chased and bred. Instead she lives like morning air of the desert, unseen but sweet, uninsisting, bright, clean, looking into every place, seeing around corners, never seeing itself, never looking for itself.

There's no hurdy-gurdy here in the waste, there's no circus, there's no fruit-seller or fortune-teller.

There's no windmill to grind wheat, there's no black earth to grow grain, there's no loom to make linen, there are no fish to catch.

There are no musicians, there are no dancers. There are no women here, no women!

Wife, I miss you, sundrenched one, lost in our silence. I don't understand where you've gone. We should hold hands and swallow the earth together, then I wouldn't have to miss you. I would leave Christ here and return to curl up on your belly and listen to your breath.

Yes, I prayed to my wife. So Christ walked away. He walked between the grains of sand. Each grain offered a different path, innumerable paths are in this pathless open place, but he'd already chosen. While I looked at all the other directions and wondered, he walked across the sand quickly. I followed him a while, a month I think, my wife three steps to my right. I followed the receding savior, accepting his path even now, losing all other paths, grieving as if I were killing a million gods at every step.

Two things were in motion: the orbit of my wife, whose body sent out coolness in this heat, and basted my skin in solace. I felt her drinking the heart of the nectar, producing the breath of birds. And the moving-away lost orbit of the receding Christ, the vanishing, flying, unreached, unachieved spirit of my Christ, who drew me on with the wound I'd cut into his ever-absent skin.

He didn't stop. Never once did he turn back to me. I couldn't imagine his smile. His smile was hidden under a mountain of flowers. His word was drowned in an ocean of flowers.

As I followed Christ by day like a wife, at night I prayed to my wife as a goddess. I said: This pain, isn't this you? You're the beauty that draws me and the pain that pushes. Does all nature submit to you? If a fur-wearing squirrel finds a soft mate he can't catch, does he suffer at night, does he stare at himself and wonder? Does he ever say *I wish I never met her*? Does he say *I can't decide if I want this pain to end*? Does he watch the pain like an enemy, and learn to live with it, can he still bury walnuts while excruciated with love?

As I followed the son by day, in the mornings I also prayed to the father. I said: Why didn't you ever hear me, God?

Why were you missing from the sky?

Do you not exist? Am I alone?

How wide is this world?

How long will I follow my lost Christ, whose body moves away so quickly, whose body is light because his faith in me has been discarded?

Amen.

God. Gnawer, bone-grinder, name-eater, you make all this life, you'll devour all this flesh, the whole city of flowers you'll eat. You'll eat these mistakes you made, these millions of searching faces, millions of articulate minds. Where there was a life of pain, you'll eat and not even leave a stone carved with the word "DESPERATE." You disapprove our skin, need, wonder, confusion, striving. You press us together, you fill us with the need to create more flesh. Then you kill it, and you make the gravestones roll down the hills, and the chiseled lettering wear away in the rain, you make granite soft, memory into smoke. We try to carry it all, we cycle through religions, yet it's you who makes holy books molder in piles like cut flowers heaped on the ground.

I loved you quietly, I didn't want to offend you. Give me tedium, I asked, settle me. Pre-kill the young man in me, give me love as security, a mild nothing. Send me Jesus as a picture, not as a man. Let me build crosses with him in silence for far too many years.

What I want now is to drown in beauty, and Jesus runs away because I chase him for his beauty. When I was young, I could catch him and hear his words confused, disordered with rapture, and forget thought, forget my name, I wasn't even there to experience the loss of myself. Jesus was destroyed, Jesus was everything. I was lost in devotion to one who was lost. We each sacrificed ourselves to a beloved God who was the act of sacrifice. Pain absent because God suddenly absent. Then you returned to me, with your son, claiming credit for my joy in transcending you.

God, you God I loved. Put out your hand. Let the wandering-away body of my Christ be stopped on his path. Send an impregnable wall of honeysuckle across this desert, to turn him around so I can see his face.

And if he shows me his face but won't look in my eyes, send a mist to soften his heart. And if he won't soften, send hail in a storm so he'll shelter in my arms. And if he won't come near me even then, it's because he knows my heart is with my perfect wife. Let him mark me down for Hell. Let me be the first person he ever hates, I'll still escape your judgment. When I die my body'll live in the lake of her belly, without you. We'll have children who won't be angels in your heaven, but gods themselves. My eternal small wife will come to me wrapped in a sheath of light, and you will molder and darken and lie still and vanish, forgotten like men all are, you'll be forgotten in man's image.

At another ridge, I saw my Christ stop at a bush and take a small orange fruit that was offering itself to his mouth.

Coming up to him, I saw him eat, and in the softening light of the late sky I saw his face, pleasure on his face just like all emotions showed on his face, directly and without guile.

But after I had this loving thought, I looked for my reward. His face turned away. He wouldn't praise me for a thought.

I saw the pink-orange fruits on bushes all down the ridge. I yanked at one, but it refused.

The fruit then darkened in my hand, and started to complain to me.

It narrated the cycle of its life: a fruit, a seed, a new bush, a new fruit.

I yanked harder, saying "Give me the taste of sweetness," but it wouldn't. It said, "I'm tired of the cycle of rebirth! I'm different, I'm a whole universe. If I die, the universe ought to die. I want to ascend to the heaven of music and fruits, the heaven of perfected fruits, the heaven without trees, fruits without seeds. Your stomach is not my heaven."

A fruit on the next bush complained about a small scar on its skin. Screaming, it said its soul was warped, and it cursed its fate in this meaning-less world.

The whole ridge of fruit started shouting at me, "See me, see me, my skin is out of round! Imperfection everywhere! Your world is a filth-pile! My mother was plucked, my father was eaten! Colors and wind and sunlight and awareness, it's not enough, not enough!"

One fruit weeping threw itself from the top of its bush, cursing the sun that ripened it and the rain that filled it to bursting, wishing for all this to reverse, dreaming of greenness, hating pinkness, calling on its infant bud-self to return, calling on the faith it once had in the meaning of sugar.

If I leave my wife for you, Jesus?

If I leave my wife behind as I follow you, she'll never abandon me. She'll wander the desert searching for me, shouting painlove that sounds like poetry. She'll be filthy, an unlovable attribute in women. She'll lose all the pride God hates.

If I leave her to trail along after my ephemeral Christ, heedless of my wife who is immortal, then her pain will be complete, and she'll search, lost, her body caught in the brambles of this world. This world, chunks of dirt, thorns, sand. This world of snakes and rats, this world of living in holes. In this world she'll be tangled, she'll be caught, her body will be embraced.

But even then she won't be her body.

She will be God. She is God.

Her walk will be her tongue, her hymn will be her breath. Her embarrassment, her awkwardness, her stuttering feet, her filth, her rags, they weave a hymn that can make the sun and moon into identical twins who sit still, their bellies pressed together, not breathing.

Her skilled dance was a weapon, she's put down her weapons. The bangles on her wrists and the kohl on her eyes, her anklets and her lip paint, she dropped these at my feet. She will love, she won't extort love. If I leave her for Christ, she'll sing "I wish I'd never met you. When, Spek, when will your eyes die from my mind?" Later she'll sing "The gods themselves have died of love. How can I complain? Spek, I'm honored by your honeyed cruelty."

She keeps the Absolute in her eyes, and the Absolute hovers around her. So she can walk out of the city of flowers into the desert wearing no clothes at all, and men won't interfere. All are welcome to look at her body, because her body isn't anything, her body was discarded by her husband. White as jasmine, devoted to my name, wild, she scares men away.

She's my wife in her heart, she crosses the desert alone, in pain and naked, passing between stones, singing to me. "Why don't you show your face?" She begs the birds and the silkworms, the monkeys and the fiery sun, "Where is he, my Spek white as a book, sky-inhabitor?" She has me confused with an indefinable god, my unreachability has given me divinity in her blood, she feels my divinity as pain.

If she chooses one wrong path between the dunes, then she'll wander forever, her head will fall from her shoulders, her flesh will be given to insects, and only her words will live, as every word ever spoken lives on. When her head falls from her shoulders, her words won't see it happen. They'll speak themselves on, tumbling forever, yearning.

Each grain of the desert finds the dune it belongs to, and each dune helps in holding up the sky. She passes between a dune of heedlessness and a dune of anger without climbing onto either. She settles her body into a dune of permitting, which sighs to feel her back against it. Written in the sand are words that never blow away, right where everybody can see them, STUTTER, CLUMSY, MISTAKE and the words have a single heart drawn around them all, and the heart is beating.

She sings *At this very moment he may come* and looks everywhere again. *Let my love for you die here. If you don't come to me now, or now, if you* don't come at the next now, I'll kill my love and bury it here, and forget where I buried it, and forget burying it, and forget. Where are you Spek?

When you appear I'll control myself, I'll look away, I'll mutter, I'll be thinking of something else. I'll be the strong one you admire, I'll be like your Christ, better than your Christ. I'll be your love itself, I'll be your eyes, I'll be your smile, let your Christ be your frown, smiling Spek.

I move slowly with my head down because I'm walking without you and the air of you is thick. The pain in my blood is these jagged bits of you that tear my veins. You must be thinking about me, Spek, to do this to me.

I'm saturated with you and you're not here. You're the two worlds, desire and selfhate. This pain that has joy in it, this flower with a flame, it comes from my clumsiness, my bad luck. Teach me the graceful walk through your heart, the walk that won't kill me with every step, oh Spek teach me.

My friends can't understand. My mother is upset. My former lovers are furious. There's nobody I can talk to, nobody I can ask. Spek, you tell me, how do I save myself from you?

This household god of yours, and this Christ son of his: you told me they withhold their love from you. You said my face was like a sacrifice to God. But I don't love this god. He taught you to snare women, as he snared you. He taught you to forget women, as he's forgotten you. He taught you to ignore the pain you cause. Then show me how to sacrifice my pain to your naked idol. Show me how to crucify pain, beautiful Spek.

I used to wake up happy. The world was soft and I could hold it easily. If I loved a man he was in love with me too. He was flesh, he had a voice and he spoke heat to my ear. Now I'm in love with an illusion, and I wake miserable and don't see beauty anyplace. You've pulled all the beauty into yourself, terrible Spek.

What does it mean that you're "seeking"? where do you need to go? My pain is everyplace you can look, my pain is in the bowl of the sky, a broken sky falls on every head. There's noplace you can go that my pain won't gaze at you, begging you to kill it. If you walk into the future, my pain is there. If you walk into the past—but the past, before you appeared to me, was all ease and beauty. Will you infect that beautiful sky too, Spek, will you desolate even what I remember?

In my fragile heart you live raging, a black god killing creatures who gaze into your eyes. In my evil heart you live as an attributeless miracle, you sing light from your indescribable throat. I dreamed of my hands reaching for your light, and you woke me, Spek, by stopping my heart.

I could have been a mother, whispering sounds to a believing face. This is a mistake, isn't it, singing these words to your absent eyes? I should create a new song instead, a song of sobbing, a song of a vibrating heart, and give it to anyone who uses his ears with love. I could have married an unworshipping man with a face like flowers who would dance with me as I danced with him, who'd feel no guilt at my name's joy. This is a mistake to speak these words to you, you who won't dance, you with absent feet, you who are all name, only name, Spek.

Shedding my song you wouldn't listen to, shedding my eyes you looked away from, shedding my dancing that didn't move you, shedding my opinions that bored you, shedding my awareness that didn't warm you, shedding my body that couldn't keep you, shedding my mind that didn't interest you, shedding my heart that was invisible to you, what is the container for this pain, and what would this pain have me do now, without a self and without you, Spek?

My mother grieves because her daughter is damaged, is distracted, sits talking about a man's eyes and hair, his voice and words, and his absence above all. She tried to teach me to protect myself, even when I was small she warned me against this. Now she's furious at my beloved, who has demolished all her teachings. Will you still teach me, mother? Show me how to hate Spek, the way you do?

For others, it's like you don't exist. They don't know you, they're free and lost. So they don't understand what's in my eyes. This darkness here, it's a picture of you, it's the dark watcher within me, the black ball at my center. This little black object, source of my pain, I would not give this treasure away to anyone. But I'll give it to you, Spek, to rub its perfume on your body.

I touched your body and before I could say "How strong, how soft, how vulnerable, how radiant," how this and that, you'd already become a million Speks in my blood, and another million in my heart, and a million million in my mind. You may abandon me but I have no shortage of you. Did you know you've been singing me to sleep at night, and waking me in the morning, Spek strong and soft?

If I lie here long enough I'll forget you. I can't possibly think of you every moment, this can't go on. If I lie here without you I'll dissolve, and the blob remaining won't be a girl, it won't know how to miss you. If I lie here I'll evaporate, and rise on ninety different breaths of air, and join that cloud there, and drift across the earth. But even as vapor I'll still know you when I see you. I'll fall on you as rain, Spek, I'll soak you to the skin.

My heart is too full. If I met you now, like this, there'd be no room for you. If we ever merged together, how would there be space on the earth? We'd have to find another place to stand, a place without pain, we'd have to become formless, an idea, a banner with a symbol on it. We'd have to hide in the space between the seconds of time, or we'd crowd everybody out, Spek, the way you've crowded me out of my own breath.

I know you're married to a god. You're following your Christ to the edge of time. Your goodness and loyalty have helped you flee the filth of my body. You married the father in heaven, you love the son on earth. But what about HERE, in my head, in this infinite world of invisible images? Will you hold me in your arms here, at least? Will you marry me here? Our wedding will take place hidden between two atoms. Nobody will know, nobody will see. Out of the whole vast plain of earth, our marriage will be the size of a small jewel-box, the size of my mind. The honeymoon will hide here, within me. Here in my head I can give you Saturn for your ring. Here *are no boundaries, here we span the ends of the universe. Here in this other place, in this hidden place, let us hold each other. Here in this place, Spek, let us kiss.*

Spek, here is your prayer at noon, here is your bright prayer to the gaze of love. Today you know you're the center of the world. With my fingers I paint the adoration of the sun on your face. In this prayer you hand yourself over to the sun. Pray to me. Speak to me.

I can't hear you.

You're evaporated? I'll evaporate, your god can't see vapor. Did you pray to him so much he's breathed you in? Then you'll be his sky, where all the aloneness of the universe is kept. He's alone everyplace, you can't console him. He'd destroy this world to avoid loving it.

I'm vapor, I drift around you, I'm scent of orange that feeds you, I'm scent of cedar you can climb, I'm scent of earth that never ages, I'm scent of...where are you?

Why did you leave me?

My heart is the lion, and you pretend you're a tree. I climb you and loll on a branch, you feel my soft belly stretched out over you, you close your eyes and wait for me to go hunt somebody else.

What will you feel when I'm really gone?

How will you live at night? Will God hold you, sleep with you, shake his head over your beauty, sing into your hair? Will he awaken with you every morning as an infinite pair of eyes an inch from your eyes, saying yes?

Don't evaporate forever. I won't wait forever. The world puts beauty in your arms, but you have to hold it, you have to hug it to your chest.

If you kill me by saying: "Beautiful sin, I abjure you," then I'll remember you as my lost husband who couldn't step into a river. Time will flow me past you. Someday you'll dive in after a different love. Or someday you'll die on the bank, kneeling, thanking your god for the beautiful intricacies of thirst.

This look on my face is only in this instant. If you close your eyes now, you'll wait eternity and never see it. You'll die never seeing it. It's not in heaven later, it's here.

Take my face in your hands.

No, I won't give you up. Evaporate as fast as you can, idiot, I'll just pour myself back into you. As you destroy your being, as you turn into mist for God's nostrils, I'll supply you with more self, always more.

Your eyes up at the sky yearn for purity, trying to transcend this terrible flesh, and yet I see what you're doing. You still hold your mouth open as I pour an ocean of scented honey down your throat.

God is eternal endurance. When your night won't end, when there's no creature in the world who knows the need in your eyes, when you give up on time as a bringer of sweetness, and you wait in the desert and even death won't come, the desolation of time, that's the eternality of your God.

THIS is eternal without endurance. When you touch the skin along my jaw and feel a chill in the roof of your mouth, and in the arches of your feet, the sun stops. We hover, dangling time from our wrists on a thread. Our minds are this mind that doesn't think or tell stories or remember the names of things. We don't even sing, since songs are embroidered time. To merge takes an instant. At the heart of the instant, this world is over.

Where are you tonight. Why do you insist on time passing. It sears my womb.

Why did I meet you? Go away, be unborn. Why did you show me those eyes.

God of Spek, kill him, or marry him, or uncreate all his ancestors. Pry him out of my skin.

I see my husband kneeling in the desert. I want to protect him from snakes, I want to fold myself into flatbread and slide under his tongue. I want to feed him dates that have never lived on a tree. I want to feed him honey that rose from the bottom of the lake.

If he is the boy who brings milk in two buckets, the brown hill he climbs is like a pregnant belly. If the sun sifts cinnamon into his hair, then there's no language, no war, no angry knowing.

You're the most fortunate god. There is a soft abyss in him for you to fall into. Depthless submission. Look in his eyes as he gazes at your sky body. His eyes will melt you.

Ohhhh his eyes, what he imagines in your sky as he gives himself over. Your stars, glittering treasures, your trance-making gold lights and silver lights, he feels heat in them that's not from your heart, only from his. God in him is infinite kindness, love, adoration. He's revealed himself and calls it you.

I won't steal his soul from you. He must come to me. He must first try to suckle on your spiritual rubies, he must try to eat your feast of ideas. You don't pour into him as I do. He must starve first, in your arms.

Every day he wakes in your desert; every day you refuse him a quenching rain, and he tells himself the blue of your sky is a gift.

Every day his loneliness pours over your absence and creates the outline of a companion for him.

As he sleeps, the shape, the companion, the bodiless statue, it dissolves again.

Every day he has to whip up new clay out of dust and sunlight, and pour it on to your name so he can see a shape that might be you.

But this morning, Lord, when he awoke and again there was no rain, he felt thirst as thirst.

This morning, he remembered you, and so realized he'd forgotten you.

This morning he heard himself remind himself that your scorching sun is loving warmth.

This morning he touched the image of you and found no body within it.

Now it's noon. He's bereft. He reached into himself and cut out a red cord and held it up for you, and you cursed it for sin. Now he can't put it back in himself.

Dead in his hand, a snake that was him, the part that twisted within him every time he heard the word "love," the writhing he felt whenever beauty hurt him.

Tonight he won't sleep, yet he'll see a dream. You don't put dreams into him. Where are you?

He'll taste in a dream your bitter absence, and wake in the dark and pray:

For sixteen years I said, "I've found what is permanent in the world."

Unmarried to your flesh, Lord, I was only your employee. I lived in this church built by unbelievers, ate food paid for by doubters.

Every Sunday sane men would enter the church to feel their eyes touched by our strange faces, by holy pale creatures who didn't drink or work or entertain guests or listen to music or dance or argue, but who kept to our stone halls and ate dour offerings or didn't eat, if our Lord preferred, and who prayed constantly for the death of our desires.

The sane, healthy, ordinary believers would leave their offerings of grain or fruit or clothing. Their mammal joy would be subdued and they'd think how death comes irresistibly to all, how death is truth—they'd feel that and then walk back out in the sun to their carts and camels. And thank God they would make jokes as they returned to life, they'd laugh into the face of the flower-scented sky.

They were free, God, you couldn't have them. Out in the desert, your wind mourns their bones it'll never blow through. The desert wind loves bones.

Lord, I spoke sermons to those free men, I tested their souls with words, to find one who might be desolate enough to embrace you.

I won't make sermons any more, I can't be trusted. I'm wrong about everything. I'll love you and try to listen. I'll pray and try to make my prayer match the flesh-stripping wind. I'll make a silence worthy of your desert sun.

The sun here doesn't give color to the cheeks of young girls. Here the wind will catch the striped garment of my wife and rip it upward from her body, her sweet garment will sail high. And your sun will burn the purple and orange dyes from it, so it lands bleached and humiliated, soft, almost liquid, ready to rot and feed a malign mute desert plant.

And my naked wife will wander in circles, her eternal power draining from her. The sun'll watch her the way men once did, harmful watching. Instead of loving her in detail, the sun's watching will subtract from her arms and legs. Light is all colors and she'll hear all the music at once in cacaphony. She'll lose the name Qurratulain and become a keyboard of darkening colors, as her face melts from the earth. Your sun wants her dead and she'll agree.

For sixteen years I baked in your oven, trying to become dry and hard enough to serve you, worthy to carry you a drink of water. My wife touched me with one drop of water on her fingertip, and I collapsed back into my original form, my wet clay. I begged her to paint her skin with me. She's a jug of water the size of the oceans, but now for me, for you, she's willing herself dry. The sun's firing her clay, she's crazing her own surfaces as she vanishes. And any man who ever loved her, he knows those colors as music in her. Now they'll be permanent, Lord. Permanent things are all silent. The wind will blow at her sweet form, testing for bone.

For your sake I walk away from my true wife.

Something created in her a ferocious fire of belief. Was it you, Lord? She believes in you more than I do, for my sake. She followed me into this desert to enter your grinder alongside me.

Lord, I promised you long ago. Even against the infinite pull of love I'll be loyal to you.

Loyalty is when I hold the empty husk of the pomegranate, and insist aloud I can taste the seeds. My Lord, the juice of this fruit is invisible. The law of a jealous god is dry as sand.

Since you know all, you know I hate you.

I loved you once. In those hours I didn't have to *be loyal* or imagine *faithfulness*. Then, for years longer, waiting to love you in those moments you permitted it, I kept faith. Love would return.

Finally you defeated me. In defeat I was loyal, since nothing human was left.

You waited till I'd burnt out the light in my eyes. You waited till my life was nothing but respecting you, the corpse of love. My need hollowed out within me. Then you sent my wife, you hit me with a tidal wave.

You once held me in a dream of sainthood. I might have withstood this then. But the saint died in my belly.

I never did stand on one leg for a thousand years, heart closed, breath held, concentrating on your light. I didn't pray so unceasingly that you writhed in pain from my devoted heat.

Is that why you destroy me with this woman's terrible eyes? Don't blame her on the Satan you made. Don't blame Baal or the gods of Egypt or Nubia or Rome. You, creator of sulphur, creator of magma. You who fills clouds with a flashing light that kills, you did this.

If you shred my heart, my soul won't be worth having. I'll jump into hell. Hell is sweet water. It's a place without you.

Hell deep as her eyes. And your desert's a surface, all the way down. You offer powdered bones.

No, I know. The empty vessel you call it. "Pure" absence. Blind white death.

Oh then press the sun into my lap, burn her out of me. Her lower lip. The heat of her hair. No no no no no no no.

If you're in this world, appear. So I can spit on the weapons you use.

She pulled me out of the city of flowers for your sake. The whole city had become one of her breaths. If I breathed the air around her shoulders, you would die. You can't live in that air.

Then thank you for this wasteland. Thank you for dried thornbushes. Thank you for the snakes that skulk and live on nothing.

She loves me. She's stayed near me, thou absent one. Her feet touch this same sand, she makes your desert a lake of honey.

Her toe is more to me than your eternity. You demand too much, and pour nothing.

Let me be like you, and thrive in emptiness. Let me inhale your infinite sterility, become living sand. Let me understand flesh and water and color and music and the hum of a girl's heart as flavors of poison. Make my pain worse. Let sweet things hurt so much I'll flee them forever and become impervious as a jug. Fire the clay of me till I'm so dry my skin rejects honey and wine, light and air and water. Till I can hold those things without tasting them.

The night I met her, overwhelmed by your cruelty, I lay on the high parapet of your stone church. I curled into the stone, with my back to the moon, and prayed you'd let me sleep forever.

You wouldn't. Of course not. When have you shown me your mercy? I only asked that you let me sleep, and roll out unknowing into the air, and fall in darkness, and die dreaming.

You scorch me with your creation, but refuse to let me burn to ashes.

I was willing to die with my face turned away from you. On the narrow ledge I lay on my side, with one arm and one leg hanging over the edge, in your thin uncushioning air, my forehead pressed to the stone of the temple, feeling below me the squares and fountains and statues and windows, the city in its huge stone awareness. The *fact* of my true wife was everywhere. She fills your stones with desire, they cradle, they breathe.

Did you, Lord, create that woman? Isn't she beyond your ability? Isn't she beyond your understanding?

She's stronger in me than you've ever been.

The wounds she makes in you and in me are deeper than your son was ever wounded.

Your son was supposed to be my path. Christ's name is mildness, in him we smother our intensity, in him we dissolve all our need, he reaches into the center of the heart and cools the flame, turns it to a scant eternal drop of milk.

But with my body pressed into a stone ledge I met the Christ as he was. He who slept in death for three days, needing to be left alone. Exhausted by bitterness, forsaken by you. Shocked at your absence, sleeping the pained sleep of exhausted love.

So touch me not. I'm asleep without sleep.

You, God, you did this. You dared enter the blessed body of Jesus, the scented mind of Jesus, and broke my Christ's silence with a whirlwind. The silence I loved in him became a song of your absence. Wickedly you made your own son weep. You made him wither a tree in anger. You made him die in blank despair. You took his peace from him, so I could find misery. You wanted me inspired by his pain. So you gave me a true wife, so I could need her desperately.

My God, my inward God. Holy Spirit, I don't know what you are.

I only know your face by your teeth, your gnawing.

I only know your eyes by your sudden cruel moves, the speed of the trap door you open.

You've slit my skin from belly to mouth, but you've never put your finger on my flesh. Why shouldn't I turn to this healing goddess?

God of every lack. Are you only sadness? Are you the craving for death? Are you my disease?

If you came on the wind and I breathed you in, if my body caught this illness of you with my breath—then, Lord, hold your breath and be trapped in my breath, I'll blow you out onto the wind again, and you'll be carried to the sun, you can bake yourself on the sun until the cruelty's burnt out of you, along with your terrible perfection.

God, if you came in the water, so I drank you in, and needing you became my blood and my heartbeat—then <u>increase</u> my need for you, <u>increase my fever</u>, drive me into even worst wastes of this desert, so in the heat you'll rise out of me like steam, your mist will finally leave me and enter a cactus plant there, and the plant will live in hallucination, dreaming of itself as the cactus that flayed heaven, the cactus to whom stones and seeds sacrifice themselves, the cactus to whom all creatures bow down weeping,.

God, if I caught you in sound, if you came into me in the womb through my mother's kind voice, if you infected my mother's voice so I needed to hear it every minute, so I could never sleep without the love of an an invisible being—then I'll walk out in the storm and let your thunder deafen me, let it shake my liver and bones and shatter everything in my dreams that can hear, every hair that can quiver for a sound it needs, every goosebump that listens for a whisper. Let thunder wipe me into a hairless, earless, skinless stick, so your incomprehensible arms won't wrap around me, so that your unimaginable legs can't wrap around me, and with a humming, with a crackling, with a buzzing you'll fade from me and go to the moon to be reflected, you'll bounce off the dish of the moon into the ear of some other mortal fool, and leave my ear and my heart.

And if you were inborn in me, Lord. If you're my flesh itself, Lord. If you're my brain and belly, every drop of me—then let's go together and enter the chopper, we'll enter the shredder, we'll enter the sander, we'll enter the fire, and we'll be shredded and filed down and burnt to powder. Then we'll go back to my mother, who'll swallow us. Inside her we'll shrink to a million drops of gall, and a thousand drops of gall, and ten drops, and one drop. I'll knife open the wall of our one drop, and you will leak away.

And that'll be the end of our dancing, creator god.

And if you're not even a disease—if you're the essence instead, as you imagine you are—if you're the meaning and motive, as you boast you are— then you won't care if I spit on you. My spit, mighty Lord, is also you, it's you. You don't need me to grovel. I'll just be one speck of you that hates itself. I'll un-name the sound of my name, I won't be you or me any more. I'll be wrong, I'll be your waste, I'll fall outside you.

Darkness is the place of freedom, I'll run there. You'll put obstacles, but I'll run there. You'll cover the ground with sword blades and cactus needles, but I'll run there. You'll command your faithful murderous against me, you'll fill the path with stern bishops who worship the cleanness of the holy knifestroke. When I run past them you'll surround me with angel de-luded faces that'll promise everything. Then blackmasked faces to threaten eternal torture. I'll pass them all and run. You'll forbid it, you'll make me fear it, you'll even ruin laughter by sending sophisticates to mock that dark quiet place, but I'll run there laughing.

You'll tempt me, lord of devils. You'll remind me of your offer. The saint you promise I can be, the sweet icon, the placid holy soul, the beloved, the wise, the holy man people think themselves unworthy to beg salvation of, the one whose life is told in hymns, the man whose fingers are already designated as relics, whose name is a prayer, whose face is a spell, whose ex-istence is more pure and more perfect and more gentle than it can possibly be, I'll break that saint's bones between two boards. I'll hammer his famous haloed face on an anvil till nobody can ever pray to it. I'll scorch his gilded fingers black with fire, so they can never again awe an audience with theatrical gentleness. I'll feed his tongue to the gulls of the beach, so it's torn apart in squawking screaming, and can't ever speak its stupid name loudly unto the sky. I'll drag the saint behind me like a sack and fling him into the oak tree, and the tree will grow through his mouth and prevent his famous sermons, the tree will grow through his heart and stop his admired piety, the tree will grow through his eyes and keep him from finding the eyes of those who adore him, the tree will grow through his ears and stop him hearing praise, the tree will grow through his brain and consume it as greedily as you consume our yearning, God, and he'll never be able to tell lies to you again, or behave as if he's the favorite of your son's apostles, or look darkly on his own incomplete fame as a form of exile, or consider himself bitterly neglected if anyone else in the room is allowed to create a holy silence. He'll never again pray to you, Lord, for more cunning to achieve even more fame and honor, all for the benefit of man's eternal soul. A tree will possess him, and it'll be one mediocre tree among many, nobody will ever find it to kiss it as a relic. It will live the long life of a tree, watching great temples being built and collapsing again, hearing people shout out their urgent prayers and angry visions, then only thirty years later not hearing those people talk any more, instead always a new jumble of voices, saying "no, me, me." Such a tree is doomed to be cut for wood to carve gods that will decorate walls of houses built where the forest was. Gods to then be thrown away one by one, as people change their minds about which god is their favorite. And the famous saint in me, your puppet, your echo, will not live eternally or even for a moment, he'll never live, he has never lived. The world will build new temples, and the low-born who keep these temples swept will expect praise for the good job they've done, and if they don't get their praise, they'll suicide.

God, you didn't flow down into me from heaven. You were born in my chest, crowding my heart. I left my own animal path for your sake and followed you into a pathless blank like a bug blown by a great wind, like a dead leaf learning humility in the waste. Every time I spoke normally about color or time, I sinned. Every time I ate food and tasted it, I sinned. I rotted your river by drinking a drop—I fouled your air by sucking a mouthful—I chilled your sun by stealing a ray—I never deserved these gifts.

But to soften my sight of you, you gifted me your son, like handing over an ancient flower. There are many blossoms in your world. I lived in a city where every girl was decked in strings of flowers. Flowers floated in the fountains in every square. They grew in every window, they washed up on the beach. Perfume was in our dreams, perfume in the milk and the rice. Yet you brought me the memory of a dead flower, and I took it, excluding every other.

In that city I found my savior. In every street I walked with him.

The Christ of my own hollow space, with the dark eyes I always wanted a wife to have, with dark hair in thorned braids that made me dream, with fingers that thought and quivered as he prayed.

My forever Christ of sun-scattering shoulders, who holds his anger back with a delicate red thread, and though insubstantial still walked with me throughout the city, he saw and knew human hearts, felt our small needs, generous like the rain-bearing cloud.

He who stood out in a city of thousands of gods of great beauty, gods all offering flowers and accepting hymns of utter love and humility and eternal embrace, gods all smiling fiercely or making their heartstopping grimace, painted wooden gods walking along the beaches on the warm days and collecting the worshippers who most need them, warm bronze gods walking barefoot through the streets trailing miasmas of incense, resonant clay gods sitting in the windows decked in pearl garlands and gold bangles and silver rings to catch the eye and seize the heart—the Christ who walked through Egypt understood these gods as beautiful children. Christ whose wisdom and kindness could defeat ten thousand maidens giggling the name of Hathor, Christ whose flowering face in the moonlight defeated the flowers of all the mountains to the north, Christ whose dark eyes in the daytime made the night serene with knowing, Christ whose smile in sunlight made the moon feel weightless peace. His name was Christ Jesus, and my own name was Spek, and we were married every day in our own form of time, following the pace of our combined breaths, praying to each other in words and gazes, under a canopy of our own thought.

Lord God, this is how you kept me apart from the world for another season.

And at night in my stone church, my breath a choir of fear, I tried to sleep, in the merciless roar of the stone.

I prayed to your son for peace.

He was invisible as all dead men. Invisible as you. In my bed I was alone. In the night if I could feel his presence at all, I felt you behind him, your hand burning on his shoulder. He was only your emissary—if I gave myself to him, he would turn me over to your wrath, your judgments, your hell, your never-approachable standards, your inhuman certainty.

This city is swamped with gods. But men change their gods the way they leave their wives. They yearn for a love they can't imagine.

Most of them leave their wives to drown lost, diving and searching the soft ocean of women. Only a few, the blessed. have wives who <u>are</u> an ocean.

I'll leave you, Lord, before my life is over.

I know why you never appear on the earth. It's so we won't get used to your voice and face. So we won't look through you as we ache for a sweeter god.

Christ, my Christ. Hear me, in secret. God took your heart from me. What if he now enters into my sanctuary, my hidden soft world, my sacred cloud of kindness, the eyes of my wife? With God looking out of those eyes, I'll have noplace to be.

Christ, your brow is beautiful because bent in anguish. Your eyes are beautiful because helpless, hurt. No evil motive can be in your heart, since you suffer. No harm can come from loving you, because you're not strong, you're the wish for air in the sepulchre. You're the memory of sunlight.

If I don't protect you from God's anger, you'll be destroyed in the sun. If I don't soothe the pain he inflicts, your pain will corrode your kindness. If I shield you from bitterness, and rescue you from his heaven, then you'll belong to me, you'll cling to me in gratitude.

Jesus, escape with us! We'll give you our lives, we'll join together within you. I'll take the knife and we'll cut away everything in us that belongs to each other. God will receive our dead flesh on the ground. Let him toy with that.

I hear my wife praying nearby, her voice is hoarse and ragged with disbelief, but she prays to your name in my name. She's lost me, you've won her.

So now come to us, come away from that heaven. We'll enter your heart and become part of your flesh. You won't see our faces again, our trivial faces will vanish from earth. We'll become very small, too small to touch each other, we'll combine to walk the paths of your blood and body and heart. Our lives will pass into you, you can rename us whatever you want. Spek and Qurratulain will vanish into you, we'll look out through your eyes. We won't be married but joined. You'll carry us. And our stupid flesh will be taken from the table, it won't be here to be tempt us to gorge on each other, it won't be here to stink in your nose. The hands that wounded you by touching each other in love, they'll be smaller than dots within you. Praise you, we will be spirit, we won't wound ourselves again, we won't know the grip of our bodies.

In you, Christ, where God can't reach. Where God can't speak. Where God can't see. Where God can't torment. In you, in you. Protect us. This is our love, this is your tremendous love. Thank you, mild soul, purest heart.

Within you our thousands of paths will each be scented differently, each lit and colored differently, each with its outcome in bliss. When we start out on a path, that's the same as reaching its end, all everytextured pain and sweetness in the same instant. Our agony of not-touching will be washed in your blood, every drop of you an embrace of us both. And our joy will flood you so that you would never wish, as your father does, for praise.

And all the nights you've left me alone, all the death in me you've caressed, all the obliteration I've yearned for, all the weeping she's done—that will be only the snares and tolls and passwords and mazes and darkness on one path out of our thousands of paths. And if we follow that path, we'll float over the snares and see only their beauty. We'll understand you at last. We'll taste the beauty of that destructive path, the beauty of the exploded god, the beauty of the weeping woman, the beauty of the baffled priest, we'll see all the beauty that comes of terrible destruction, and we'll float above it and reach the end in an instant and smile, and dark will be light.

I hear her praying to your father. She's distracting him for us. Come now, come now, while she prays:

God of Spek. God of my husband, of my universe.
Infinite God. If it be your will.

Forgive me. I was never the goddess. I'm nothing.

Give this filthy woman the right to speak.

Give this gaping vacancy the right to beg mercy.

I don't dare invoke you. I'm only woman flesh. I can't command the LORD OF WORLDS to appear before me.

Indefinable, incomprehensible, infinite God.

Who's neither this, nor this, nor this.

In this desert I'm lying on the palm of your angry hand. I'm yours to crush.

Eternal punishment blossoms from your eternal righteousness.

I haven't earned your grace.

By chaining myself to this stone pillar, I'm drowning in vainglory.

I'm trying to blackmail you. To shame you I display my little yearnings before you. Like breasts and genitals to tempt you to love.

I don't direct your heart. I can't command you to wither my flesh. I can't beg or wheedle you to demolish my desire.

Don't free me of pride. Pride is my body squirming for freedom. Orgasming its disgusting wish. I can't tell you to change a speck of my body. I'm your creation.

You put desire into every bit of me. You made my womb yearn. You gave me a mind that leaps a thousand miles in an instant. Right now my mind still crawls through my husband's body in the city of flowers. The tongue I pray with is filthy with pink yearned-for flesh.

You built me in paradox, and goaded me into this desert. You command me to solve your riddle.

No answer is in me.

The only heaven I know is sacrifice.

I have nothing but my soul and body and lifetime to give, I give them.

But you don't appear to me.

I speak your name, Father, you don't appear.

God, God, God, God, God.

Mercy mercy mercy mercy mercy mercy mercy mercy mercy mercy mercy mercy mercy mercy mercy mercy mercy mercy mercy mercy.

Because I haven't sacrificed my mind. I pray unceasingly, but my mind doesn't enter any bliss of ALL-GOD.

Not even the bliss of your wrath. If I could feel your lightningbolt, your rain of sulphur. Instead you leave me alone with thought.

I'll give you all I can. I vow I'll bring my husband's soul back to you, that's slipped away.

God, if it be your will, grant me the right to know your command.

I've told you every memory I have. You've heard the stories of all my sins, except the ones I'm too stupid a creation to recognize.

I've confessed to more than I remember. More sin than I even believe, in so young a woman. I burnt for you my most jouous memories of live, and destroyed the core within me.

Forgive my husband for my sake. You'll have his love through me. I'll show him your mercy in my eyes.

In the daytime, praying for mercy—for MERCY—I stare at this high rock I'm chained to.

On the other side of the rock is my husband, praying. So the writings on the rock have become his voice for me.

See the carvings here. At night I touch them unknowing. In day I stare at them baffled.

Incomprehensible lord of all, since you are the lord even of all other gods, did you make these marks with your finger?

I kiss the meaninglessness of this one-sided stone. I kiss your speech to me.

I kiss and bow and scrape my forehead and bleed on the lines of carved saga here, in your language, your unsayable tongue.

77

I weep and rub my wet cheek against the pictures carved on my side of the stone.

I try to understand. My stupidity is like a woman who walks through stone. Stone is wiser than me. In the night I wake and wail and bang my head into your words, know it as a door to my husband, bite my chain till my teeth ache.

What's this carved man, looking at the sun? What are these signs or words below him, made of fish and birds? Why are his face and fingers long like one who melts in sunlight?

And along the bottom, why do you carve that so differently?

What is this bird stretched all across a sky? The kneeling man beneath, what?

On the far side of the stone, where my husband is, I refuse to go. I'm ashes. I burn myself with the fire you lit.

I'm feeling, trembling, begging stone. Carve me with commandments.

You created this lust, the infinitely deep bog of flame-scented bellies.

My husband of the desert, who prays and meditates and screams your name in a whisper, he attacks his belly with prayer.

And you harm his beautiful body with your absence. You won't simply reach and caress him.

Your mystery. The bird you carved in this stone sky, is she lust shining, giving earth its children, giving us our children, even as she leads us to hell?

The dung-painted man with long stone fingers, will he put his fingers into me in your name?

How do your angels bear the sight of pale perfect angelflesh? Why cook us in this sweet stew, and refuse us the taste?

God, you God, what is this fury in me? Is my anger the holy spirit, the ambrosia of fire?

You despise your creation. I would smite your world for you, if I had your fists.

Why not destroy us, here in our filth? Why don't you burn this sickness out of the earth?

This feeling I have for you, this furious terror, this obliteration before your face, this is love.

Love splatters my blood against the sky.

Love annihilates me, love like exalting hatred.

Love fury fear, love righteous anger.

I understand you, insane God.

I alone understand you.

When I was a woman among men, waiting to meet my husband, you sent me many bastards, liars, tricksters. For your pleasure you sent me men who used the word LOVE every day.

You sent me blasphemers who dared touch their mouths to the words I LOVE YOU. They spoke it nakedly to my face.

Those words. The most powerful in any tongue. These men spoke them and became my owners. They injured my heart with that curse.

Once I watched a man's face while I was holding him. God, while I was holding his beautiful face in my hands, while our skin was actually touching, he said "I plan on being famous one day."

I watched his eyes and ached for this world.

The beauty you put into him, I watched him dump it on the ground.

The beauty you created when you created skin, who in your world adores it without fear?

The infinity in a spine, the eternity in soft ribs, the abolition of time in one finger touching one hip bone.

I danced alone, overwhelmed. I loved so much, I hoped so much. All my life I touched into beauty, closed my eyes and hoped to feel my breath stopped in another's chest.

Beauty, Lord, the beauty you make. I'll love you forever for this. I loved men for what their skin meant. Lord thank you, that was you speaking. You'll deny it. You're crazy. I know your heart through the skin and eyes and voicemusic of women and men. Your heart is bliss that doesn't feel itself. You don't know your own beauty.

Love is terrible pain. The worst pain you make.

You dropped me onto this earth inside-out. Anybody, anybody can touch the center of me. You can.

I'm another of your experiments. It didn't work, Lord. I can't bear to live.

But thank you for this beauty pain every day.

I'm infinitely reduced by your infinity. I let you into my arms and you zero me. I worship you. Will I swing in a dead circle around you forever? Float in the salted lake of you forever?

If you keep absent it'll be your death. This is a prophecy, spoken by the mud in your path, spoken by the nil of the space between your toes.

Appear mighty one. Come pick me up, I'm a rag on the ground, take me and use me to clean the gore off yourself. How many of the disappointed did you slaughter today.

Before I knew you, Lord, you filled my heart so I'd love my friends with an ache, so I'd want to marry all my schoolteachers, so I'd run burbling through the yards, so I'd fall out of a tree on purpose to feel the earth, so I'd want to enter the sun and touch its inner life and never stop seeing something to love.

I came to the city of flowers, and every day the city exploded in me.

Your creatures had overrun the earth to carve and weave beautiful objects, and pile them up, print them with shiny colors, adorn them.

The singers and builders and streetsellers of tinwear were pouring their lives out, creating moments of fire in the mind. The blue stripe on a man's sandals would cut into my heart.

All this they did was for love and for food money. If I bought a street vendor's shiny dazzling god-painted glass bowl, he could buy scented rice for his mouth to love, his belly and whole body to rejoice in.

I touch that man's chest in thanks for this glass bowl existing. I look into his eyes. I'm scented rice to his belly.

And watch as his eyes get angry, furtive, frightened, cruel. All the bright bitter intensity you taught him, Lord. The terror of love.

He takes me to a private box of stone and plaster, specially built for humans to sleep and touch bodies in. Private, unseen by all but the gods of the Nile and you.

I watch your eyes, God, as they watch sin. The sin of this man's anger as he orders me to undress, as he pulls off his own clothes he hates, to reveal his body he hates.

His body demands food, costs him money, squirms with desire for women he can't buy, writhes alone wanting, seeking love in the touch of himself, finding no love in that beautiful touch.

I'll be his drug today if he'll allow it. I know he'll only use me to shout into, use me to resent all the hours of his life when I'm withheld from him. I know, I've seen his eyes.

But if I could touch his body perfectly, even once, he might know. Beneath all the pain words that fill his head now, all that wanton and fuck and whore and secret and filth, deepest in him might be devotion.

Let the drug of my fingertip on his jaw splash beauty down the inside of him. Let honey fill his thighs and belly. Let heat strum his chest, let his toes feel this fingertip.

Let him wait. Let him give himself a gift of me. Let him forget time, let him forget his language.

Let him feel my touch at his sex as worship of all that we are. Please Lord, let him know your meaning when you call the sunrise.

Let him know I have a soul that can tangle and merge softly with his. Let him forget to wield power, let him feel the power of your creation in us. Let him taste heaven that pours from our breath and blood.

Into the furtive look in his eyes, I'll sing gentle nonsense. The meaning of the song will be the moisture of my breath against his ear. Heat is your heart, Lord, breath is the pouring of love.

And his anger as he takes hold of me? Oh Lord, if it must be, then let it be expressed beautifully. Let him at least be obliterated in his anger. Let his rage fill heaven, let him overthrow you oh Lord. Let him become God as he throws my body onto his narrow bed. Let him walk the universe as he grips my back in his fists. Let my back be infinite. Let infinity be in his hands.

Let his sex know every boy and girl and man and woman he ever desired as he presses it against my backside in this heaven-overthrowing fury. Let him feel he possesses all humanity when he possesses me. Let him feel this as a transgression against reality. Let him destroy the reality that has deluded him. Let my flesh be the gate, let my softness be the touch of God, let my soft yielding places be overwhelming beauty for his mind. Let my interior be too much beauty for his anger. Let his mind lose its grey patterns. Let color and honey and light enter upon his darkest place.

And into his orgasm let him pour all the tears he can't shed. Let the barrier break. Let the need to need blossom in his belly. Let the love of love be tangled in his chest. Let him never come back to himself. Let him be another.

Let him sleep now, in dreams of this.

Let him not awaken to his day, his time, his job, his fear.

Let him sleep forever, so his dreams create him.

He dreams of you, Lord, in me.

There is a fireball in the sky of this incredible planet. It's my palm held upward.

A woman holds the sun in one hand; with her other she enters him through his belly, her hand sending forth blasting light.

His body is full of light and he's terrified.

He can't breathe, or he would beg darkness to return.

In this light he feels the demand to live. Now that he can need, he must chase.

He sees a boat. My hand has gripped the center of him, I'm pulling him into this boat.

Lord, yours is the boat, mine is the boat. Lord, yours is the sun, mine. Ours is the belly, the terror.

Lord, you and I mix light with dung, we let mankind choose which to eat.

In our flesh forever become light, he's weeping at losing the dung body he hated. This light is death to him.

The boat, it must be death. And he gathers all his time around his head, time whirls in his head like bees, and he tries to scream away this obligation we've put upon him, an obligation to die and live.

So when he wakes up he's in an ordinary room, where light and time sit stuck in the walls. He's so relieved to be noplace, as he thinks. His relief comes down upon his head as a misery, a dark helmet he'll never remove.

My body offends him then. My body's a cruel rip in the dullness. My body's a softness through which he could still reach beauty, and beauty might come reaching to hurt him.

He beats me with his rootlike fists. He curses with the voice that can sing, the voice that can whisper, the voice that can tell poetry to the delicate ears of short-lived listeners. That voice you tuned, Lord, he uses to scream. Like God.

His screams are a granite cliff, they have your vast frenzy my insane Lord. In sacred error he knocks me to the floor. When he kicks my head I see your blue stars explode into being.

Lord, I am a created mammal, and I will worship my maker with all I have: my sex, my heat, my skin.

Lord of heat, thank you for heating us. I know they're wrong about you. You can't want me to cut my body away from my soul. You knew what you did in making me. You made my soul out of body. Any man who loves my sex loves me, and you.

Is LOVE written on your barrier stone? These marks and pictures, could they invoke annihilating love?

If I can read this stone aloud, will you appear to me in your body?

Will you crush me in love? Will your love rip the thighbones out of me, strip my spine up through my back, break open my head like a pulsing egg?

Your messengers, your men with flesh rods, with tongues that easily speak the words of destruction, these men chained me to themselves. Then they walked away free.

Lord, I forgive you. The day you sent me my true husband, you forgot to pick at my wounds. Instead you sent me the messenger who is your message. I saw your eyes in his.

When he said I love you I lost the strength of my knees, that was your voice. That flood was yours.

I forgive you. You gave me your eyes that day. Only once. But it's everything.

I'm yours. I know you love martyrs. Before I married, you killed me with endless messengers. You killed me with love that boils up in incomprehensible, wordless, dazzling hatred. I died willingly.

Now you've sent my husband, who will not relinquish you. Are you the spirit of stone?

God is who makes me guess.

The lover who reveals nothing. Even when I pray the right prayer to delight you, only the light around me changes, not you yourself.

One morning there was a forest, a lake, geese, a rock, and I lay on the rock and let the sky heat me. Should I have torn my eyes out instead?

Is everything I've seen on earth, sin?

All the beauty you created? Am I here to hate it?

I once touched a piece of Chinese rubber, and felt the smooth skin of it. Was that evil?

A man poured milk from a dipper over my thigh, and my eyes closed. Should I have resisted?

I was speaking words before I can remember. Words are my heart, to me. And red stain comes from your berries. But if I paint words in red across my belly, and it says <u>He turns me into a river</u>—must you be jealous? Yours is the river, don't you realize?

I won't eat till you answer me. Your own food, offered by fearful pilgrims who walk a mile off their road to place fruits within reach of our chains, and never speak to me or my husband, never show their eyes to ours—I won't eat these sweet treasures without your voice. Just as they won't look at my bare skin, even though I'm just another piece of fruit you ripened.

To win your heart I'll struggle against fruit. I'll have dreams of figs, wet and purple, smeared across my belly, crushed against my closed mouth, bursting with seed, fatter than the Lord of Heaven.

Dates will cloud my mind in ashes, though once I ate them and loved them. Now they'll torture me with my desire. I will think of you as starved, Lord, in need of my pure unfed skin. But when I pray to you my mouth will still taste dates, mere sweet earthly dates, mere ephemeral kisses of creation.

The things of our world are sublime, I've always been devoted to your body within them. Now I must turn away from you in them, since my beloved has turned away from me.

I was a fig in the palm of his hand. I was honey on his lips.

I love you in Spek, Lord. He is a true sign of you.

Build a low stone temple and I'll enter it, to hide my body from your offended eyes.

Build a temple with rib bones I can climb, I'll cling to the low ceiling and join you lying across the sky, facing up, avoiding a view of our loveliness.

Look at me when I talk to you.

Please, your face, there must be some of Spek's beauty in your face. Show me the place under your lower lip, he has God in his curve there.

You held the brush that painted his lip. You're deceiving us with your holy book about brown dust and grey stones. Lord, become the woman who whispers you what to paint. Lord, worship your own belly, so I can feel you in mine.

When you tell us to wither our desires or face Hell, when you tell us to starve ourselves of this world—you want us lovesick. I am lovesick. I can't stop thinking about you. I see the shoulder of your servant Spek and I can't breathe your air or eat your food. You glow out of that place.

This is dancing, orbiting. I want to merge with you, but I have to dance around you instead. My body is ready to be consumed, but instead—eyes, yearning, lightning, gestures, the need that twists me. I sing hymns, chant words that make this pain so much worse.

Then destroy my body, you maker of the men who won't take, you inventor of moisture that dries up. This world is an evaporating swamp. The nastiness of men's hearts is only their yearning to be purified of the stink I've been calling beauty.

I'll cover my eyes, and your moon will be destroyed. If I destroy the moon, you will be my light.

I'll cover my ears, and your birds will all die at once. They'll drop out of the trees and never hit the ground. They'll never have been born to create sin, or take joy in empty song, or have greed for vile red worms. They won't ever have existed as lust-ful creatures feeling air under their wings as they soar, loving the illusion of being swallowed by the sky before dawn, the way I hover here before dawn beside the body of my husband. Sun comes to expose the truth.

I'll cover my mouth with my hand. And my lips won't feel the softness of my *hand, and my hand won't feel the wet of my lips.*

I'll cover my mouth and be silent. In my mind I'll pray: <u>I am unworthy of</u> <u>your mercy</u>.

I'll die, I'll accept your gift of death.

Nobody will know I'm praying. They'll call me crazy whore of the desert, filthy strumpet chained to a rock.

They'll throw rocks at me, and I'll close my eyes and feel that sweet sting, that touch, the pinch from your destroying fingers.

I won't eat, but keep my mouth closed. If rain falls into my mouth by accident, if a bug crawls down my throat as I sleep and feeds me on itself, then that's your will.

I'll cover my sex with my hands, and not feel the honey or the heat or the soft fleece. I'll never again feel the bliss of the sunlight that spreads within us when we sin. I will be rock, free of yearning.

What I called beauty in your world, I'll know for filth and vileness. Since the world is vileness, I'll turn away from it, and love you who is pure blank.

What god has ever been invisible? Absence is such incomparable perfection. Oh why did you make a universe? The rotting clutter only interferes with the gorgeous void of you. Skin without clay, soul without body, sight without eyes, sorrow without tears.

This self, she's my enemy. She wanders, stupefied by the colors, dazed by smells. She wants to crawl into beauty and stay there. Her words repeat: beauty, belly, honey, need. On her hands and knees, lost in fields of pollen, her head down, drunk, unaware. Decay smells sweet. My Lord, you wait for me so patiently while I croon and moan nonsense.

Sinfully I adore men's bodies and women's bodies.

Sinfully I drink music, the human voice of sex.

I roll open my skin for anybody to write on, and I don't care what they write, I love their words.

I drip ink from my mouth, needing a body to write on. And when I'm in the magnetic state of love, I write scribbles, not even words, I make pictures, I draw lines that try to focus this power, that worship this quivering, lines that mean yes.

I pray to anything but God. I pray to the river to make me liquid and pour me into the mouth of my beloved.

I pray to the cow to make my breasts pour milk so every person I pass can taste sweetness in their mouths.

I pray to the shoreline to make my skin a thousand miles long, so men and women can live there forever, and even God's hermits can lay their head on me and feel utter peace.

I pray to the air to make me present everyplace, brushing every thigh on earth all at the same moment, entering every mouth, caressing every neck.

And when I first heard of your existence, Lord, I prayed to every other thing in the universe, I prayed to everything that was not you. With all the devotion in me I begged to become you.

So I could reach into the heads of every human on earth, and pet their minds until they tremble and purr.

And reach into every body on earth and touch its core with my finger that's always wet from sending the rains.

And reach into every plant heart and animal heart and feel the vibration of need, the hum that is music and eternity.

And hold each soul in my palm and love it and love it and love it.

Such was my lack of understanding, such was my blasphemy, such was my obscene greed.

Your Hell is a place you designed, or rather you permitted sin to design it, the way the desert is shaped by the winds.

Yours is the Hell-shaping wind, and you are the creator of even sin. Blasphemy was born in your mind before it could appear on our little rock.

If bees make an insane music of life, swarming by millions on a treetrunk, then the sudden destruction of all bees would sound like all their music in one chord.

I'll deny the vibrations of bees.

I'll deny the smell of every wet patch of ground.

I'll send all color up to the sun to be burnt white.

I'll send all warmth into the center of earth, to be tombed in black.

I'll turn everything toward the one, you, the zero.

I'll empty myself of this glittering trash of a world, and scrape the hair off my scalp with my nails. My hair that dances in the breeze, that shows itself nakedly, that undresses the wind and exposes it.

I'll still have a body, but it'll be below me. I'll simply look up.

Lord, simplify me to nothing.

Translate me from this language of things into your speech of silence.

Turn my worthless love into yours. Turn my breathlessness into exaltation of your presence.

I adore your absence. This is your greatest poem.

I must shut up. My life is from you. I am small.

I must not praise you in my words.

Teach me to pray, to exalt, to revere, in a way not stupefied by words like prayer or poem or absence.

I'll wait for your language.

Lonely.

The spirit.

The heat.

Stones are bread.

Corpse is a shrine.

Prayer is a gnat.

Creation dies.

Throw myself down the mountain.

Dash myself on stones.

Here, this morsel. Feed on me.

The furnace I am will remain, but you will have my self.

Fill my furnace with what will not burn.

Spirit, fill your vessel.

Spirit.

Vision of descending stones.

Stones to fill a furnace.

To kill its heat.

I'll inhabit the interior of stone.

I'll breathe stone.

Eat stone.

Let stone have me.

Pure, dead.

Forever, stillness.

Simple. Empty fullness.

I am your bride, and slave.

...Am I your bride? Do you love me devotedly? Of course not.

You have no wish to be me. Of course not.

You don't feel the urge to climb into my body and feel my skin from the inside.

You don't wonder what it would be like to feel what I feel. You know it,
without desire or mystery.

You don't want to get so close to me that you are my flesh, you are my
feelings.

You don't wonder about anything.

You aren't of the normal gods. You've never been drunk, or ambushed.
You've never come down to flirt with an earthly woman as she rows a boat across a

river.

You were never attacked by other gods, and had your phallus severed and buried in a hidden place.

You are not of the god's body that could be cut into seven pieces and scattered in rivers and mountains.

You never stop the world and lay a fog on the land to become invisible as you make love to a mortal girl.

You have no needs.

I am bride of one who wants no bride.

I'm devoted to one who's kind to me, who gave me life, but who doesn't need me.

You're a father, not a husband.

I was born into a house, and locked up, and it was your house, an ungraspable cloud of dungeon. Deep voice that knows all.

I didn't understand existing. But you brought food, and you spoke, and you were the container of kindness. I was grateful, Father, but I feared your strength.

Once in Egypt a mathematician loved me, and spoke to me of his love of my body, its tangents, its vertices.

He loved that I looked precisely like all women.

He loved also the predictable stars, the predictable dawn.

He loved me to speak in words he knew, words he expected. So I spoke those words for him.

Lightning didn't frighten him, because he understood it.

He proved in a diagram that you exist. He said you must exist or existence would be unpredictable, unpredicted, unprotected, indefinable, incomprehensible.

Indefinable incomprehensible God, this man understood you.

He could hear your voice, far off, every time he fell asleep. He couldn't understand the words, and that made him so happy.

In the night he opened the curtain, and as the moonlight crossed my thigh slowly he gazed, praising your name.

His relief rose in him like dawn, that my body was the precise size of itself, and that there was no mystery in woman.

He loved you truly, and was truly your brother. Neither of you have need.

But now my husband, made of love, filled with need, has found me. What path can I walk with my beloved into you?

If my true love and I never touch each other, do you grow stronger? Can you get any stronger?

If we abscond with each other, so that you lose our souls, so that we drown in sin, will your universe be deranged?

We're apples on the tree, bumping each other, forming a tender spot, a bruise.

If we rot, and fall, and are eaten by a red jackal, the jackal is your creature.

Satan is your creation. You dyed him that shade of red, and measured the fur at his hoof. We can only be food for your creation.

Lord, you have millions of apples already.

We're supposed to fast. You never fast. You devour praise, prayer, souls, every moment.

Stop. Desist from wanting more. Do not want us. Let us go.

Our souls are immortal. We'll be punished in eternal fire. But when he touches into me it's you I feel in me singing Yes.

Lead me there. Shine in me, speak loud, sing clear, let me hear all your joy in my love, all your joy in his beauty. Make a joyful noise unto us.

I love you most when I wake up and feel him, and feel the shock of you again enter my body as you howl TAKE HIM INSIDE YOU AND MAKE CHILDREN so that I double over and writhe with the need to keep your paradise roaring.

God. Inexistent sorrowful God, listen:

I can't pray to you, God, to release him. Every day men leave you this same *way, every day they become angry and give you up.*

Your creation breeds, ignoring your anger. You hoard love, you who should know that one single loving pair of lips is infinite.

I won't beg you. Instead I pray love to drown you.

Let God realize that Spek should forget him.

Let God forget God.

Let Spek realize that our eyes are God.

Let me become the mother of earth, and marry Spek, and our tiny son become God.

These prayers are only language embraces, idea kisses, I can't touch them. They drift like silk with no color.

Spek, my brother in Christ, enters me with the prayer word for entering. I feel it and don't. I exult but like a memory of exulting. I orgasm in a bed of words, where words wrap and taste me, but never grip my skin.

This will be our life then. He'll love me like a stone carving of a longing face. Because men are limits, because each man is trapped on a path, because all paths are circular and none will spiral away from its order.

I'll say yes. Anything, yes. On my knees beside my stone I feel the words he sends me every night, I hear devotion and children and a thousand names for love.

The names for love dissolve the world.

Lord, the names for love dissolve you. If you only could have been loving. We offered ourselves.

But when we forgive your wrath, we're dying in you.

When we tremble, we're dancing away from you.

When we dare not speak your name, we're dreaming of love's body.

When you built heaven and hell, and suspended us between them, you taught us hovering.

When you created time and sharped its edge into a sword, you taught us hovering.

We hover in each other's arms, stopping time.

You can't defeat us. You're a name, a myth, a limit. We won't be limited.

You can't scare us into obeying. Obedience is never love. We'll only love, we will only love.

You made an earth with creatures desperate to love. You made us more powerful than yourself. Lord, we'll kill you if you try to keep us from touching.

I love him.

You'll try to kill him. You'll use time on him, he's half-old now. You'll rob his soft skin to cover your footstool. I can't prevent your hand from reaching into him every night, stealing beauty. But my love will go to my husband. To him, not to the night thief.

Oh this woman, Lord, this woman in your belly, who creates with her whole heart, who loves to experiment with new mixtures of flesh and plant and clay, who just smiles when you try to scour the land with thunderstorms, when you try to erode the colored stone. She travels everyplace your fingers have furiously scraped, and kisses the ground there and sprouts a million new seeds.

All she does without explaining, just pouring new liquid life every day—can you ever stop her speech? She is your self's body, are you ashamed of her? We want to pour ourselves over her, and abandon you of the smiting hands and furious brow. You should learn from her the sacred self-obliteration of making.

Because you're wrong. Death is not beauty. If you set me into the black sky, and revolve me around a red star for a million years, so I start to feel the curve of eternity, I'll still dream of the skin behind Spek's ear.

You'll pluck his eyes someday. But now I've seen into them. If I have a soul, it's made of his eyes.

You float in the dark, bitter, and boast of your infinitude. We can't cure your loneliness, we're too small to give you love. Love between equals, love as love is.

You make eyes like Spek's so you can destroy them. You want us scared of you. You demand we love you, lest you take your gifts back.

You've only taught us to do without you. His eyes are eternal.

I hate you, they are eternal, you don't exist.

His eyes are God. His face is God, not you. I worship his body, not yours. I praise his voice. His hair tangles your universe. His breath swamps your starlight. His voice outwarms your sun.

He's a flash of light but I see him. His smile will vanish but I feel it throughout me.

My fingers and feet are at the two ends of eternity, quivering in his kiss. No other creation exists. He's our universe, I'm our creation. Spek is the sky, I'm the earth. He holds me everyplace, he floats me in his airy hands.

There's no room for your glowering eyes. We're busy. Don't stand in our light. You didn't create this light.

Go. Find love. Find your consort. Shouldn't there be a goddess for a god?

Consult your belly. Split open and look at that wonder, Nature we call her, Realia, the heat you oppose. The sculpting hand that invents fur just because softness is sweet. The womb within your belly that creates startling gifts, like plants we can chew just to fill us with bliss.

Wonder in a plant juice. Exaltation in scents. Meaning in the depth of eyes.

Her creations have attributes, a roar of colors. What color is your skin, Lord?

My skin is pale cacao. I name it for a plant that gives pleasure. Spek's skin is pressed flax. Lord, did you ever feel fabric pressed against your skin, and rubbed gently there?

Look at her, spinning within your belly. She hides her fingers, but creates at every moment. Her skin's every color, her body writhes across all creation.

She's pleasure, beauty, love, we want her, we adore her. And you, your miracles are time and anger. You're our defeat. Be defeated now. Let her clothe you in skin.

Let her give you a body.

Touch her without judging. Touch her without time. Let time alone. You are God, you can do that. You can change, you have that power.

If you marry, Spek and I will worship the two of you. But embrace her as the miracle she is. Don't shout rules at her. She's so much greater than you.

She'll marry you out of pure joy. Because she sees the beauty in even an unlovable invisible desolated solitary jealous god. She'll create new clouds that remind her of your eyes. She'll deepen the thunder till it sounds like your snoring. She'll make a moss nobody sees, a moss in one deep cave, in one tiny place, just to memorialize the texture of your hair.

Let her brush your hair. Close your eyes! Feel what we feel. Love us, for the first time, truly, your heart joining ours.

I tell you these things and you're silent.

In my life as a vacancy, I knew a cruel man like you. When I was soft, I knew a soft man who hated my softness.

I was infinite in my skin then. The route from my hip to my thigh was longer than all your rivers.

A god could die of thirst while trying to climb my breast.

My toe could dig at your horizon, and tap at the moon there, and my hair would obliterate the other horizon and tangle the sun so it couldn't rise.

And your earth would moan at holding my backside, and your sky would rush down to inhale every pore of my shoulders.

I will not describe the Caananite man who knew how to tread on all this soft creation, who battered my head and loosened my teeth and felt nothing of the pang in my eyes.

I won't describe him. You created him.

So I'll describe you, Lord.

I see you. You're soft, beautiful, and angry. You speak of love every day. You mistreat us who love you.

You want dignity. You're so easily offended. So quick to punish.

You can feel joy, but you get furious again. You throw us out of Eden. You won't share.

You want endless, ecstatic, pouring love. That's what we want. You want prayers and adoration. That's what we want.

You close your eyes and feel us adore you. You need this so badly.

You live in need, alone, vast. You enter us, you enter our hearts and bodies, just to listen to what we're thinking about you.

You spy on your birds to see if they're joyful at your creation.

We'll never be good enough. You won't ever adore us.

We're just like you, but you terrorize us so we don't dare know.

Do you ever feel ease? Can you melt, stone god?

Have you ever entered time, the crystallization of plummeting?

Come enter time. Death is here, but be as brave as we are. Come, fall.

Forget yourself once. Forget your greatness. Give up your furious inhalation of prayers. Just close your eyes.

For one piece of duration, let all prayers be judged perfect.

Allow everyone into heaven, everyone. Especially the adulterers. Dissolve sin.

Here, here I am, a girl who sinned because of love. I broke your law for love. Here's my heart.

Love me for the beauty of my sin.

Love the ones who fail you so badly they transcend you. Love the ones who need you so much they find you in any touch of skin.

Come join the praise in these sweet bodies, who meet you in themselves.

In the whorehouse, God is meeting God.

As a woman, I glowed in Eden. I felt you best then, when I never knew you.

Before I heard your name, I held your true flesh in wonder. I felt your sky *fuck your earth, in every embrace.*

The taste of cinnamon curd, the light when rain and sun combine, the awk-ward boy making a song that's got no meaning except the gorgeous vibration of his chest. These were you.

I know you, invisible one, haughty one, you hate being seen. You'll end up de-stroying me.

You'll ruin my skin with wounds and emaciation.

My beauty, that came from you, my beauty that's touched with your face, you'll eat it. You take back every gift.

If I see into your creation, will I become immortal? Is that what scares you?

"ONLY I AM IMMORTAL. ONLY I HAVE THESE FEELINGS."

We all feel what you do. We love you with your own love.

If I love a face so much that breath stops, heart stops—that's your secret of immortality. That's your private self.

What's the harm, infinite one, if my beloved and I live there with you?

Do you want me to hate your inner voice, to rip it out of me? You let one drop of beauty fall into my mouth, then forbade me to drink.

Was I about to touch the flaw in you, the limitation you hide?

Was I unworthy to hear the sigh of your tremendous breath finally relaxed?

We're so hurt by the touch of love, we murder and revenge to escape it.

Your awesome anger fills us. You watch us die. But watching us die, that doesn't please you either.

You think you weren't meant to be pleased. You think happiness would be a sin against yourself.

What would a happy God even be?

Would you praise us? Sing hymns about us, thank us?

We know how to be happy, though it's hard. Won't you try?

Allpowerful one, rock of frozen joy, come to me. I'll hold you in all your depths and melt you.

Tell me what's wrong.

What have you lost? What was taken from you? What was refused you?

Oh dearest God. Lord, my Lord. I think I know.

I'll hold you and tell you a story.

I knew another man. When he was small, his mother left him. She felt such intense love for a new beloved man that she broke your law.

She tied her little boy to a large stone, at noon time, a little boy tied to a stone.

While she tied him there, she was praying to her new beloved, he who was born to overpower her whole mind. He whose flesh had the strength of your wrath defied.

She was praying to her new husband, her next husband, her future husband, her rightful one. And she left the little boy there, waiting to be rescued by his father, the old husband, the despised rejected one.

When the boy grew up, I met him and saw his face. His face was silent as your night sky. His eyes were infinitely far off.

Dearest God, where is your mother?

Where is she right now?

Do you remember her? Were you too young a god to remember?

Was she Eden before Eden? Was she the warm voice you heard when you first opened your immense eyes? Was her voice why you invented air?

Oh god of love. Was she love? Why did she go?

Tell me. Do you miss her now? Oh, I am so sorry.

Love, tonight I'll sleep right here, in the moon-shade under this rock. I'll be right here if you want me.

You've never come to me before, except as misery, fury, terror. But, tonight, come to me as a name.

Whisper me a single name as I sleep. Put one sound into my heart, sing it in my sleep.

Tell me her name.

I'll wait, I won't dream. I'll sleep waiting for your voice. Whisper your mother's name.

I'll love you if you let me. If you won't blame me. If you won't feel I've wronged you.

I'm not your mother, so don't be angry with me. But I'll love you in her place and never leave.

Tell me her name in the night. You'll be free.

Tell me, then curl up beside me, and I'll hold you as we both sleep.

Your first sleep in an eternity.

Your breathing will slow at last. I'll whisper to you "You've done nothing wrong, dear one. You are good. I love you. Let the world alone, now."

Then if you still love anger, be angry, I'll be fierce in my love of you. Anything for you. Our anger will be the great glory of creation.

These weeks, when I was alone, crazed from lack of joy, screaming in the desert, you watched me. I didn't hide myself from your eyes.

I'm the shape of your mother, Lord. I'm the breasts of earth, the ass of sky. You see me naked, yet you protect me.

I invoked you with my body, and you clothed me with a husband's eyes. You caused a saint to appear, with eyes warm as a long blue cloak.

You were gentle that day.

You can be kind. I know you're kind.

Before you sent me Spek, when I was a woman quivering in the city of flowers, I cried, cried. I was shocked at your creation: that a woman yearning has no power to invoke what she needs.

I said: may he appear. I would have ripped apart the clay of me, to press it into his clay. I said: may he appear, make him appear.

you tell.

No sacrifice to you can lead me to your skin.

I know, I learned what you are. My husband is a man who believed in God, and prayed to him all his life.

He was married to your son, the Lord God, he was destroyed in your son.

And your son, the Lord God, he never appears. You left your son helpless to love this earth.

But my husband is freeing us of you both.

Do you hear? Spek will abandon you both for a faithful goddess.

He'll overcome you, Grace, he'll overthrow you.

You have no power here, mother of God, abandoner, vacancy! Need!

I won't love your beauty. I disbelieve in your glory. Your flesh is an idea and a wish.

You're the reason God made this world as it is. You're the false promise that waits in every heart on earth.

Even your son has protected us from you. Nobody here knew your name. Wise God, I praise him for that, helpless redeemer God. He took your sin onto himself, Grace. Let both of you die now.

Grace, die out of the world.

My husband, my eternal love, is singing an endless hymn against you.

On the other side of this carved rock, my husband sings what you should have sung. He loves your son as you should have loved him. He loves God with a mother's love.

He tells God stories for his bedtime. He holds out the cup of milk, in prayer and poetry and song.

Without even knowing it, he's the father and the mother, this man, this mortal man.

You don't see him because you can't listen, you can't hear prayer. You are beauty in all its deafness. You are beauty loving itself stupidly, living in itself.

You never age. So you're never forced to think.

When any man loves you, you're a glaring mirror, you hurt each man by mocking his absurd enraptured face.

When any woman loves you, you drench her body, and flood her mind, and drown her heart, and tangle all her senses and make her incapable of any other love all her life. You'll play with her, but you'll never love her.

You've missed more love than a stone could miss in an eternity.

You've dumped gold into the ocean, you've thrown pearls into the volcano.

Idiot. Any one man on his knees to you, filled with love for you, that man was a universe of treasure.

Any woman, any man.

You took the body of my husband, Spek the priest of your son's son, and over-turned his love and poured it back into the cracked earth of the desert, and let it quench the unbelieving dirt, the uncomprehending, amazed, overwhelmed dirt, that guzzled it and left Spek empty, day after day.

Every day he forgives you, by forgiving your son.

God. Listen to us. We know your mother well. She made you believe in righteousness through her unrighteousness.

I followed my husband into this waste. Lord, I'm not like your mother, I wouldn't let my beloved suffer and yearn forever.

Spek tries to call you into his arms. Why do you refuse? Do you feel happy after you refuse?

Because he suffers, he knows you're suffering.

Every night you and I hear Spek's prayers. He laughs and whispers and hums and praises and shouts and moans. The moans pierce me so terribly I can't bear to exist. I know they pierce you.

God, in last night's dream I walked through this barrier stone, and saw my husband's moaning prayer as a spiral unable to rise. I stood naked, glaring up at your stars. Then I took up my husband's robe, leaving my footprints there for him to touch.

In my husband's clothing, his body was me. I felt his thighs carry me. I walked as him.

And in the clothing of a man I woke back in the center of this god-fucked vacancy, chained here, and began another day of begging you.

In all my life before Spek, no man I knew could feel what I feel. Not one.

I wept for them. I gasped in pain at their blank eyes.

If your son Jesus looked at you and didn't know you, and felt nothing, no anger or exalted love, wouldn't you weep?

You've been here since before the beginning. You made this earth when you'd already lived an eternal life with your mother, then another eternity without her.

But I preceded you.

When you first burned incense, the smoke rose between my legs, you caressed my vagina with wisps of honeyed devotion.

I am your mother Grace, who could restore my husband's entire body from just the shadow of his sex, who will be impregnated by one who has become a man. I gave birth to you by loving one who was sand scattered across the waters. I am your mother, I'm the hand that makes all life and strokes your belly from within.

I've come back to you.

I've come to worship the male in you, my only son. And to finally flood your heart.

I will lay you down across the curve of the stars.

You'll drift weightless on the firmament.

You'll relax your spirit for the first time since creation. The pain you refuse to name will fall away from you, and you'll finally know it was pain.

And your creation will start to drip and flow.

The fatal edges of shoreline rocks will become the liquid they've resisted forever.

The inherent properties of numbers will become a buzzing of bees.

The night and the day you made will turn into soft shadows on a face that shines secrets.

The blackness of space will take the deep light of dark eyes, it will mesmerize with need.

The heat of the sun will exhale a deep red river, wet as a mouth surrounding a finger.

Every wild forest will start to widen as eyes do when they see unbearable beauty.

Every desert will moisten like sweat on the back muscles of a dancer, and writhe gently till it's pressed tight against the sky.

And the sky will wrap its palm around the earth. You, lying on your milky arc, you'll feel what the sky feels. Against your back you'll feel the soft center of a world.

And you'll finally relent.

You'll allow the music in all molecules to be audible, so we can hear the suspended harmonies in your constantly bereft, desperately yearning creation.

You'll make yellow and violet palpable. Green and purple will soften our faces with their moisture.

Your human race will kneel, not to praise their absent father, but to look gasping down into the wet earth exposing its hips to them, her scent rising as steam, clay of every color flowing as nectar. Your creatures will finally be filled with the beauty you always showed them, but then punished out of them again. Now eternal death will just be eternal music. They'll play it backwards and laugh.

Music needn't be obeyed.

Son, you and I will walk there, where you used to wait alone. Barefoot now, you'll feel what your creatures feel. You'll have thighs that brush together as they climb through wet grass. You'll slip and fall, and feel the hilarious surge of fear. You'll laugh—all your creation will catch its breath. These stones you made in such excess, they were always bells in yearning, now they'll ring out. The air will be blue plasma pulsing with joy. You'll forget to preserve thunder, and thunder will dissolve into the touch of my hand on the side of your neck.

Son, the god in you is brittle, did you know? He'll break. You won't die, but you'll be shivered into crystals across heaven. Your brittleness has gripped the world. Its breaking will be beauty that unchains beauty.

Your right foot, with which you trod down nations, will break into a million small gods who'll give boons to plants and insects. They'll be liquid on the ground, droplet gods who caress anything they touch, they'll love without reason.

Your finger, which created all life, will drift out into a mist of transparent gods who'll settle over humans, will enter them and warm them from the inside and teach their throats to purr.

Your sex will glow and separate and become the sun that destroys and creates, that feeds creatures and melts them.

Look. It's already happened. Your sex, your hips, your belly—they were me. They made the moist worlds. Now they're a flaming goddess, and your time is over.

I'm you.

I am the sun.

This carved rock isn't here, because I don't desire it. This chain is not here. There're no chains in my world.

You, Lord, are not here. You were the idea of absence. Your creation was your ambivalent heart. It was unkind of you to create that way.

You're back at your mother's breast now. It's all over. You're being held at last. Tasting milk at last.

A mother felt you in her baby's lips, and closed her eyes and offered you her substance. Millions of those mothers.

A husband felt you in his wife's sex, and closed his eyes and offered to be overcome by you. Millions of those men.

The other billions in love with other gods, pouring all their devotion into clay dolls with fierce faces.

One man named Spek: his eyes have warmth surpassing yours.

One man can look in my eyes and stop your leaves from rustling, your stars from burning, and drown your name and voice and righteousness.

All right Lord God. Let me help you fold your strength up and put it away, and you'll hand over your creation to him and to me.

Spek, who's still praying to you now on the other side of this holy stone, because he doesn't know how glorious he is.

God of my husband, you don't deserve what I'm giving you. Lord God who presides over death, you who inhale our sacrificial smoke for your pleasure, look on me and see what I burned to you.

I gave you the hours I should spend with my beloved, who created me but doesn't want dominion over me.

I gave you days I could have walked beside him without professing faith. Our time that isn't believed belief but loved love.

You accepted this sacrifice, and never cared that you didn't deserve it. Spekgod, can I speak only to the face of you that shines the moon? You female man who promises what we wish for and nothing else. You operate the curtain, you hang the veils, you keep the beautiful distance lit with a corridor of moonlight.

Your illusions are beautiful but not necessary. We have greater mists in us.

You don't mean to. But you create the suicide of the girl who could have taught us, and we ache for her voice forever. She dies of needing. You baffle and starve the visionary boy who could have been the first to live without a god. You wreck the philosopher with the white light of fame, so he can only see good in what makes him famous. You trouble the builder's dreams, so he can only imagine buildings *shaped like money. You use the moon to trick our eyes, so we can't even see what we desire, and we learn to need the shimmering, the vanishing.*

God woman who made flesh luscious outside and invisible infinity inside. God woman who filled what we most desire with entrails.

You who opened a door into stone, so my husband walked inside. You who sent your son into my husband's flesh, and taught him worship of the absence. Who withheld your son from him, and taught him the thousand beauties of wanting. You who created us mammal, so you could watch us helplessly quiver in your storm of honey. Who plays the empty air like an oud, to mesmerize us with need. God, why did you create both memory and desert? Why have you filled this waste with moonlight, and my nose with remembered scents of sandalwood and eaglewood and burnt candy?

You're trying to teach me. You claim the window opens onto more death. You insist the treasure's never here, the meaning is <u>never</u> here. You're wrong, I've seen his face. God, release us. God, liar, dangler of dazzling hope, god of misapprehended meanings, release us.

He who was invisible to you, who never noticed himself, I noticed him. When he touched my shoulder, I loved his hand. A gesture of his gentleness was more to me than you are, supreme master. I saw him shining with music pouring off his hair. I immediately told him what your voice has never said: "I adore you."

When I touched him, only <u>then</u> you noticed him, you were furious. When I gave him solace, you sent hailstorms of guilt, you sent diseases of the free breath, next you'll send blackmailers and accidents and a thousand guardians, you'll try to send us the misunderstandings and anger of any marriage. But you are a misunderstanding, the greatest misunderstanding. You have no power here.

He was good to you. Loyal. He refused to desert you. He traveled with you upstream. You transfixed him in purity and death and Christ.

But now when he prays to purity he means my moonlit skin, and you feel invisible again. You feel obscure and neglected and unknown. Lord, you've forgotten the beauty of invisibility. You want more tenderness than humiliated servants can give. You demand love from every housefly and ant. You command us to give over our great power, to instead touch your heatless flesh with the eternal hum in ours. You want the world's peoples to hymn you in a million voices, to drug you with praise, to flood you with tears and write on the sky: We're worthless, only you, only you.

God, before you made this place, the three of us were united.

You, me, him.

I'm going to step into your creation soon, and burst it open, so we flow together.

I'll drown sin forever in honey.

Your creation is a sun, a Grace, a woman in a crown. I'll melt into her, then loins-first I will melt her.

I want to step into the body of my eternal husband. First I have to break this chain that traps our thighs.

On my crown I see symbols: chain links intertwined with human hands.

My pain colors the sun, the destruction of my desire creates colors in the sky, my exploded desire makes a purple and orange sunset. Even flung-away desire is gbeauty.

Your god-gloom overtakes the sky, and the sun sinks into the darkness on the other side of the world. Your boat's moored, you're chained in your own dark.

All night in pain my husband and I ask questions of the moon, we ask questions of our own bodies and minds, we ask questions of the manikin god we can't see in the night. We ask, what is this pain?

You snatch up that question as soon as we ask, so we won't remember or learn, so we can't know any answer that would come from our own mouths. The black part of the sky catches our question and never reflects it back to the earth.

You keep the dead with you, Lord, on leashes, and you make them operate the world for the sake of the living. The dead ones who felt the truth, they make trees *grow upright. The dead ones who had no passions in life, they dampen, they prevent the world from burning out of control. The dead ones with beauty, they design new clouds. Those who were desperate for love, they pull the sun like oxen, like steers.*

As long as I mourn Spek, as long as I'm in this confusion, the sun won't rise. But once we learn, our chains break. When we learn, we'll flow together as the river. He'll drink the mind of his wife, I'll flood the mind of my husband. Then, Lord, you can watch and learn.

Lord, when our stupidity is gone, you'll be gone. When our illusion is gone, you'll be gone. When we stop spinning, you'll lose your grip on our pulsing minds. I'll vanish into him, we won't be seen, and you'll die missing our beauty.

In every word I hear him pray to you, he drowns you:

Lord of hosts, when she offered me infinite flowers, there was noplace for me to go but your desert. I shut my mouth against singing, and closed my nose against the scent of petals, and closed my ears to music, and closed my eyes to the kingdom of her beautiful skin. In darkness and silence I felt my way to the wasteland. Even then I was delayed, because I kept bumping against her, my hands kept brushing shoulders and hips and breasts and legs. So that it took me seven days to travel the short distance from our sea to your wasteland.

For me Christ had lost his heat, within me he became only the word "Christ," a whisper of fear. In my eyes I couldn't feel the joy of his face, my ears couldn't touch the song of his voice.

I opened my eyes kneeling at night in the desert, thinking I'd see Jesus purified, simplified. Instead I saw my infinite, eternal wife, new, without ornaments, dressed in my robe, with black complex hair tied simply as a boy's, and her face like a luminous blue net in moonlight that catches and kisses gods with its beauty.

It should have tortured me not to possess Jesus. Instead I possessed a universe of gods. Christ, his entire meaning, was only one exhalation of her breath, he was only one pebble in this avalanche of her.

Then, the minute I stopped my unceasing prayer to you, I could hear with my ears. I heard Christ's voice, too calm, telling me I'd betrayed him.

He said: *I'll leave you tomorrow when the moon falls.*

He said: *I'll cross rivers too wide for you, and forests too dark for you.*

I'll travel unploughed land that confuses you, and climb mountains your mind can't comprehend.

I'll walk paths only a clear mind can manage, and dark valleys only a clear heart can walk freely.

I'll walk away from you, Spek, across a landscape of earth. Earth, not a landscape of flesh.

I'll cross bridges of rope and wood, not bridges woven of glossy black hair.

I'll travel by sunlight and moonlight, not by the light from a mirror.

I'll leave this sea behind, where flowers wash up on the beach, where men gather armfuls of dripping flowers and always want more. I'll travel to the opposite ocean on the other end of the horizon, where water is clear and shines with every clean honest creature of the sea.

I'll leave you behind and forget you. I won't carry the sound of your voice with me. I won't carry the scent of your prayers with me. I won't carry the light in your eyes with me.

My years with you were vanity. I'll sing no hymn about those years. My next years will be with purpose. They'll shine with purpose, and you won't see them. You won't know who I'm speaking to. You won't know what I'm building. You won't watch my new followers dream me. You won't watch my hair and clothing change to suit their hearts. You won't be there the day my own heart changes. On the day I'm a new god, on the day I wake up without thinking of you, and I go to sleep at night in peace and never think of you, you won't know the day.

The wound you cut into my side, I'll leave it on the ground as I walk away. The yearning in your face, I'll drop it in the river as I cross. The hymns we sang together, I'll leave them in the wind. I'll walk across the wind, I'll give all the hymns to the wind, the wind will carry the hymns out of me till none are left. Later there'll be new, joyful songs, you'll never hear those.

This picture of me, you can have it. It's yours to burn, or to sell for whore money. It's a picture of an idiot Jesus in your heart, a dead Christ I don't know.

He's just a myth, like people say. He could not have lived, because he didn't know enough to breathe, he didn't know enough to eat, he didn't know enough to walk, he didn't know enough to speak.

He believed you. He thought love was a freedom in the hearts of men. He thought air was free for breathing, and that nobody could keep the air for himself. He was wrong, so he was no god.

He believed you. He thought your prayers were real, and that they'd nourish him. He was wrong, gods can't be so wrong.

He believed you. He thought he walked toward the light on solid land, and that to walk in a straight line would move him forward. He was wrong in that, a stuffed god, a toy idol.

He believed you. He thought prayer came like birds, easily and honestly, and that if he heard a word it was true, and that it was easy to speak truth about anything. He was mortally wrong in that.

Your sins that I forgave every day, I forgive them forever, you are free to enjoy your sins.

The lies and concealments you committed every day, I forgive them forever, you are free to have secrets even from yourself.

The gospel of my life, it's untrue now, it has to be retold. But I won't gather the truth for the retelling. I won't know the real story. I won't find out what was a lie.

I refuse to learn what you've learned. I give the gospel to you and you can sing it how you want. I won't sing that story again, or listen to you sing it.

The wife or goddess you talk about, the goddess or wife you worship, I don't sense her power. She's a goddess for boys. She doesn't speak into me.

What you accuse me of wanting I don't want. I don't want the love of every creature, no. I don't want the warm praise of strangers, or my name magnified into flames and carved on mountains. My name is private, "Jesus" is mine to change, my name's for speaking in a whisper, I speak it to myself, it's known to myself. When I forget my name, I'm happier. You'll never understand. You have nothing in your hands to give me. You only take away my peace.

I'll leave you tomorrow when the sun rises, when the moon falls out of the sky.

He said all that into my quiet ears.

I tried, then I tried. I didn't want forgiveness.

Then I tried and tried:

Shining bridegroom, I said to him.

I spoke names for him that came from God, flattering names.

I tried to speak, but pain held me. During everything I said, I felt: this isn't true.

Every path in my body withered, every path was empty.

Then I broke, and told the truth, I told my anger. I said, furious: You never lived! Enter yourself first, virgin! Disappear into yourself! Fill yourself with thought! Crucify your two eyes, swallow your mouth! Disappear from your own world first! And love the world as it is!

Lord Jesus, how did your father create you and do such a bungled thing? How did he create omniscience that can't sing and can't laugh? What god makes a creature so helpless that he needs Hell to enforce mere love?

You never came to me. You've walked away from me forever, till I got sick from the motion of your retreating shape. So now, will you never leave? Erase your face and free me from you! Will your silence snare me till after I'm dead? Will I need to pray to your outline after I'm a pile of bones? Will I live an eternity of flames waiting for you to explain yourself? Will I spend eternity wishing your mouth knew how to lie to me better, so I could kiss it without weeping?

I said that to him, my first prayer without fear. I'm a fool doomed to foolishness, the prophet in the glass box knew it. But in desolation I went on and told Christ the truth, I described the beauty of my wife in all her wonders. My Lord listened without answer.

Then I wept, because I had lost my friend.

But now you will enjoy a thousand girls, he said. *You won't need me for a friend.*

You, I said. You are Jesus but you fail me here. You don't understand the meaning of a wife. All you know is judgment.

He tried: *She is your goddess, she's of you, she is you. Her sex is your Eden, you worship the sun in her womb. You see her face everywhere. She's your mind.*

You're still wrong. Your voice is hollow because you've compared her to your death and you still prefer your death. Goodbye. I will vanish to God, you can take my Christian name. I'll have her beautiful mind and beautiful soul.

I embraced my Christ and thanked him without sense, without my heart, without prayer, without God. I was only sorry for him he had no wife. I turned away from Christ, and left God pulverized, a layer of white powder across the desert, a vein of petrified flowers. Qurratulain and I, wife and husband, we wept, a storm across the memory of flowers. But our weeping was a glory. Our weeping tore the roots out of the ground and scattered the petals.

Qurratulain sang into my nerves the song of the joy of destruction. I destroyed the door of my church, I destroyed the bed of the absence of Christ. In song, in longing, I shredded the Christ voice and burnt his hair. God knew me for the first time as the thief who steals by destruction. Christ was killed again from the world, and God set off a ringing, a jangling, God set off the wail of the pimp, the keen of the knife, the hymn of the places in the night sky where no stars are.

The first moment Christ and I stopped speaking was the destruction of heaven. At a great distance I felt the city of flowers darken, like fallen fruit grieves on the ground, knowing it will only live as seed of a future self. I was the fruit whose face darkens when its shining life is lost, its memories of bud-days, memories of illusion sugar.

In the second moment of our not-speaking, the distant city lost its connection to my skin. The city that didn't love me, now it didn't look away from me, now it didn't dangle its flowers and pretend not to see me. Its streets were changed, its nerves were changed. It couldn't find me now. It couldn't feel my church on its grid. My church never was there. Christ's eyes never were there. The city couldn't remember I ever lived. A city you've never visited sits far from your mind, unless you know a woman there. The city of flowers lost its memory of my sleepless faith, and even of my sudden marriage.

Now the city couldn't say to me, we have your Lord, come find him here, we have the Christ with the thorn-plaited hair, he is our hostage. Egypt never held Jesus in its palm, he never walked its streets. It only knew him through my need, and now it'd lost me. So the church that had been the armor around my body became just a place on the ground, a lining-up of rocks, a collection of slabs, a scar in earth near a beach, a word in a language you've never heard.

In the third moment of not-speaking, a sound stopped, a sound cleared off. It was easier to hear now. A noise in my head for years, the weeping of a virgin, a noise I wasn't paying attention to, the weeping of a radiant mother, that noise stopped. So I heard it for the first time as relief from hearing it.

I didn't speak into that silence either, I didn't give my opinion of the silence. I didn't explain it, I didn't turn God's desert into an echo-bowl for my voice.

And because I wasn't speaking, the far-off church where my faith was stored, the dry floors that held my decades of silence, the storehouse where raptures are stacked to the ceiling, the circular warehouse vaults of death-yearning, the place of being-accustomed, the place where worn prayers are written out and put away again and again, this round church bearing Christ's name, this customs-house with his many faces on the door, it lost its roof. The sunlight roared in. The bible leaves were disturbed, the wind mixed it all together, sudden rain soaked the writing, the words bled out, the papers flew off into the sea, they flew on the twelve winds, they fell into the gutters, they fluttered in the sky, they went to where nobody could find them, they flew back to the bright place where gestures haven't been made yet, where love is not yet acted on, where dance lives before it is danced, where kisses wait.

Jesus was at my back when I first saw her eyes.

She looked at the sun. I saw light in her eyes and said, my Christ why did you never tell me the sun existed?

She looked at me with those eyes. I said my Lord even I exist. I have beauty and a name!

When we met I laughed because she existed, I groaned at not being married to her. Minutes I spent with her were mercury falling through the air. She was young and her hair was senseless and her tongue stammered with all she wanted to say, her eyes showed all her thoughts lithe and tumbling. If she would marry me no god would ever hurt me again.

Wife, how did I ever leave you behind? Can you hear me now? Do

you answer prayers? I miss you. All my life I tasted your skin without knowing. Last night, holding your thoughts in my heart, holding your body in
my mind, remembering the paths of your voice, knowing the heart of your
prayers, I dreamt we were kissing. Without starting to kiss, without deciding
to kiss: we were kissing.

We were within you, our name was Qurratulain, Qurratulain was
our name, we were together in a pathless place, a floor in the sky, a floor of
sky. You filled it with hovering lights by laughing, you filled it with hovering
flowers by saying my name, you filled it with paths and plants and temples
and castles by turning and facing me and saying yes.

I told you my fears and you said to drop my fears away. I told you
about my god and that I must never speak from now on, and you told me my
voice is beautiful, you said Look what you made with your voice. Looking, I
saw you reach your arm down into the living desert, it was an ocean of honey.
We sang and made this new place. Where your body is, is a loving world I
can breathe into my chest and it travels to my mind. In the place where your
voice is is all of song, the image of song itself, the language of the heartbroken
ghazal, the careful and quiet thought of the taksim, the gasp of a cymbal and
laugh of a speeding violin, the solitary voice of the girl pouring into all the
world, your voice vibrating your chest, the voice that pours your heart itself,
the deepvoiced girl voice that's free to multiply into choirs of every octave,
that inhales all the air of the world for its breath, that feels no boundary between the sob and the song, or between the joy and the melody, you are music
in its own image, music that's the thread between our hearts, music comes
from your eyes and shoulders and chest and throat and hands, from your dear
face it pours, and here in this place it's the source of all light.

When I dreamed of you our feet were free of chains and we thanked
them for holding us these years we were without each other. We floated, feet

bare. Qurratulain, transparent to yourself, vivid and glowing in my eyes, your glow surpasses all ornament or facepaint or fragrance. With our eyes we laud each other, and ask each other why we should deserve such praise from the other.

Qurratulain, light, take my life then. Pry me off this rock with your sweet fingers and throw me into the sea. Drown me out of this life where I'm struggling. It shouldn't be a struggle should it? Here in this hidden place, all is ease with you. To love you I only have to breathe, Qurratulain.

There's so much of you I can't take it all in. I touch just your hair, and you drop your head into my lap, and all your hair is everyplace, the world's treasure for me to whisper into.

Lost in you, I'm lost to the earth, all the paths I see are paths to your core. All the sky stops here.

If you're really an illusion I won't survive

If you've infiltrated my cells only to destroy me with need

If you're going to run away, and vanish from this sky, and leave me aching

Then please increase your powers over me now

Flood me with love, derail my mind, drown me

Madden me so I won't remember unhappiness, so I won't know how to yearn, so I'll believe you still love me even when you're walking away laughing

I'll fly in circles around you, and when you bat at me I'll be ecstatic, believing you're trying to pull me into you

But you. You're still here, loving me, taking my hand. You lead me into the chasm of white, and under a waterfall of milk we kneel and hide from our names.

You. Mocha-colored, stirring your skin down into mine with your soft fingers, swirling us into deepening spiral veins. This depth of yours, this capacious embrace of your tiny arms, the vastness in your gaze, the wise gentleness in your voice, where else can these have come from but a past when you struggled and learned and fought for all this self you now hold so calmly?

Each time the sun steps into my arms we embrace.

Together we draw the rivers onto the earth. You flex your neck, and I draw my finger across your back to map the torrents.

My hands as they touch you create every soft animal. Touching your fingernails spills out the reptiles. Touching your breasts churns new oceans.

Men will live and die having discussions. They will think their years away, and never press their fingers into your body.

All the human race lives in the world of this love. Their forest is our fingers. Their death is you sleeping. All music is your breath.

And among the tombs of earth Christ thundered at me, and I didn't hear it. I was gazing at a single bit of your skin, edge of your chin it was, I was lost again and marveling.

You're so small and you extend forever. I can hold your hips in my fingers, I can encompass your soft waist with my hands, but I can never reach the end of you.

Forgetfully with two fingers I'm still pressing at the wall of the heavy, huge stone house of the Lord. And now for the only time in sixteen years, I take my fingers away from the wall. Slowly the entire church slides past my distracted sparkling enraptured eyes. The house of my Lord slides through mud and crushed blossoms, and it slowly slowly slides, and over the cliff, out onto insubstantial air, the same air that's so thick in my lungs when I see your face Qurratulain, the air you weave into parks and grottos in our heavenly place—on earth this air can't even grip one house of death. I watch as the entire church slides out into air and unmade loses its place in creation. For the first time it feels itself overturned, sun shining up through the basement, eternally exposed, falling, all of it down the cliff, all of it into the sea. The sea swallows, and it's nothing. And I watch this and I see only the beauty of it, only the ancient life of air and stones and sea.

There's an ocean that covers the planet, and there is Qurratulain's toe that covers the universe.

I jumped to the end of the universe to find a flower for you, I found the deep red wall at the very end of everything, a wall higher than sight, extending forever, carved with infinite whorls of language and maps of rivers. I took one petal of a violet flower growing there and crushed it, and in flower-paste I wrote on the wall "My wife."

When I jumped back I gave you the rest of the flower. When you smelled it your eyes knew, dancer, you lifted and pointed your bare foot for me, and on your big toe I saw a tiny violet mark, the words I'd written.

Wandering the endless desert singing about you, letting my beard grow like I've been drinking bees, losing my sandals and robes, I sing gratitude to goats who recognize me as an animal who somehow has no animal pain in him, so they nuzzle me and I sing to tell them what it is to nuzzle Qurratulain, to fall asleep in her arms, to awaken and she hasn't moved, she's draped over me and her breathing balms all the air of the world.

Qurratulain's every cell of me, filling each cell, pouring into it. She's poured a million of her selves into my mind and each Qurratulain is cradling in her palms a different memory and thought, folding them to her belly and warming them. The sky's rewritten, these constellations are all strange and new. This is the sky I used to stare into and ask, when, when will it come, when will the Lord pour honey onto my eyes?

Qurratulain, small flexible soft girl the size of the world, heats honey and pours it so gently over my closed eyes. When I open them I see her through golden light.

And the butter doesn't sit cold in the sunlight, it melts and runs into the earth and is eaten.

And the lambs and cows don't weep but look at the grass and the sky and at each other in peace.

And the milk doesn't curdle, the sky doesn't blow with red dust, crows don't suddenly start screaming, our left eyes don't twitch, there are no omens at all. What's about to happen can't be either bad or good.

Spek the man, whose whole body and mind are one flame for Qurratulain, for whom Qurratulain is the promise of life, the meaning, the expansion, for whom a life of obscurity in her arms would be the pearl of achieved fame, for whom a single kiss from her would be the whiteness of immortality—Spek kisses his wife for the first time.

Here in our chariot-place in the air, here in our mild milk-saturated light, we both become the embrace of Spek and Qurratulain. We feel him hold her face in his hands. We feel their amazement, that such a thing can happen on the earth. We feel the haze fall over our minds, the sweetness, the overwhelming freedom of kissing down into each other as a spiral, endlessly down.

The whole of the lower sky is fire. We can't see the sky at all, and we hold each other. And again, forgetfully, holding each other we lose everything else, we see each other's eyes and we don't care about the desert or the flames or the anger of any specific god.

And moving circlingly across the desert come the robbers, sent to us by some Demiurge who still believes in sin. Robbers who live by harming others, those who have an anti-code. They are the ragged men who find beauty in harm, who praise love when it breaks boundaries, when it causes destruction. They are the self-adored who love floods and fires, who worship not the guest in the home but the valuable possessions of travelers. Highwaymen and thieves, pickpockets and tricksters, those of this guild join to celebrate the destruction wrought by a god's fury. And in the smoke and glare of the sky blaze, they sing the following song to Love:

Love, you never show mercy. You kick to pieces the gifts of the Magi. You leave Mary by the side of the road forgotten. You make us survive on old memories of the word. You are beyond the reach of scripture.

Love, you fall on the lover like all the sand and stone falling. You destroy his life without scruple. You devour habits and addict the innocent. You are the great highwayman, the great criminal.

Blood-covered one! Teach us your merciless ways. Teach us to devour our victims without hesitation, laughing. Teach us the joy in demolishing a marriage, so we can blacken and ruin the hopes of the strong bridegroom. Teach us to kick a house to pieces with one blow!

Collector of hearts, possessor of a vast storehouse of the bloody hearts of your victims! Show us the plant you use, show us the leaf, the drug. Lead us to the soma plant and show us how to press out the white juice with which you intoxicate your victims, so they enter the flames laughing, so they believe heaven is spinning on its axis, so they will only smile at the point of our knives, so that while they hand us all their treasure, they'll offer to kiss our mouths.

Make every man a lover, so he'll wander the forests singing the name of some girl and give up all his possessions to us, to divide between us, to buy drink and drugs with. So we can afford a drug that makes us feel we are being embraced by beauty, so we can buy courtesans who will pretend to love us, who will intoxicate us with lies, who will gaze into our eyes until we melt away, but whom we can kick to the ground the next morning.

Spare us. Do not make us into lovers. Do not make us your victims.

Let us enjoy the things of this world with clear heads. We want to be masters of the dosage. We want to decide how much we drink, how happy we become, how much of a woman we'll possess, and which woman and how long. Do not enslave us so we beg on our knees "Please marry me and I will love only you forever. Please have my son, we will name him Uriel, after the angel. Please stay with me and protect me from my friends who are all unhappy thieves. Please grow old with me and comfort me and fill me with the love of your eyes. Please say your name to me now because that treasured name of yours is one of the two words at the center of my whole existence. And please say the other word, please sing it, please, please let me hear you sing the word *Yes*.

Love, we breathe your smoke, we feel ourselves changing. Our song becomes deeper, we see life around us, we want to live. We have everything we need, we've lost our anger, where is our anger now? We have air, we don't need to take it from others. We have light, we don't need to steal it on the roadside. The air is inside us, the light shines out of us. Where are our lives now?

The man and the woman, let them be saved. They have wanted each other and given themselves and been scarred. Let them live. Let the embracing ones embrace. And let them find their home and weave glass out of air, let them create singing things out of water. Let her mouth be a chapel for music, let his mouth be a fountain of heartbreaking kisses. Let them have their wish: to give.

And the ones who embrace, let every problem they face be a nothingness. Let the thief who blackmails them also find love, and forget to harm anybody. Let their bed cross the horizons of the sky. Fill their thoughts with each other in endless detail. Let the thought of his spine obsess her, let the thought of her thigh obsess him. Let them love each others' faces so that time stops for them. Let their whispers sing like music. Let their whispers fill this entire world.

And let us be kinder to our victims than you are. Let us not do what you do to Spek's heart, he who can't even recall the name of his ex-savior. Let us not overwhelm our victims as you overwhelm your lovers. Let us not drown the whole world as you do.

Inspire us to create. We'll melt down our stolen metals and make a statue of a girl. We'll crush our jewels to line her insides with color. We'll take the best of our stolen broadswords and slit her open, so light comes into her like into a cathedral. We will climb her outer walls, singing her praise, until we reach her right hand.

And inhabiting the right hand of the created girl, we'll put our hands into her hand, lightly, and we'll feel as she moves her hand, she shapes the air, she carves water, she sculpts wind, she touches utter beauty into being. Her left leg a mosque pillar in purple and gold, her right leg a temple pillar carved with Egypt's visionary monsters, her hand is heathen, it is godless. She is the divinity within a girl impulse, manic inspiration, heated with the need to make beauty, to open beauty to her own eyes, to leave beauty on the landscape.

And we feel each quiver of her fingers as she carves and creates, carried off by maddened love for the beauty this planet churns up every moment. We know she's the earth itself. We feel all her joy just by lightly touching the back of her hand. And we are her, we are her, we are her.

Husband, I sang with you when you were alone. I watched every moment of your sorrow. As you walked, you felt me wrapped around your hips, you felt me behind your eyes. You walked through God's desert looking for the wedding everyplace. Your face was carved white birch, your head was bound together with silk strips. When you passed a cactus shaped like me, God allowed white milk to flow from it. Of course God also drank all the milk, and the sweet butter belonged to the Lord. Still, I who first churned the butter, who wept the milk in desire, I was the taste of milk on your tongue.

The cactus told you: Even cactus is a miracle. Love me in this waste, as you love your wife's eyes. Look up.

You looked up. God above you opened his mouth, and inside his mouth was every person you've ever loved, all of them tumbled together like seeds, naked, cool-skinned, golden, calm. All of them looking into your eyes.

God opened wider, there was the earth, space, galaxies, the universe, like handfuls of poppies to scoop. Jupiter and Rhea holding each other, their mouths open too, Saturn apart and closedmouthed wrestling Isis, also stones and sheet-flame, elements, ether, troubled chemicals, liquid life, airy life, all whirling.

And you saw me. One seed that jumped from God's mouth, you saw it beside your foot, it's made of uncountable tinier seeds circling other seeds, constantly reaching out, living by wanting, a need spinning forever. This germ, immortal husband, Spek, this seed, this one, only this one.

You prayed. You said to the god of absence: Your last chance. Kiss me.

Kiss me, you said, with your mouth full of lives, your fertile mouth full of the word.

Kiss the entire word into my mouth.

God with no attributes, touch me with your hands, as a mammal touching a mammal. Stroke my actual skin. You created me animal, hold my animal self naked as you made me. Feed me love or I'll be gone, flown away through your fingers into the sky.

I give you back the soul that fears the body. I'll keep my mongoose soul that's identical with the body.

Let me touch beauty when I see it. I've forgotten the taste of good and bad. I abjure clothing and nakedness both. My skin is clothed in its need. Le-

the drips from my forehead.

And my husband, as you stood and watched, with my body wrapped around you, God with a mouth was not.

His mouth opened all the way, leaving the universe with no God-body around it.

My husband, you gestured your freed fingers, and your volition appointed the firmament with our clouds of honey, soft new paths, milkbath lakes, milkbath waterfalls.

You strung eternity with marigolds and honeysuckle.

You laid me on your palm and brought me into this place, such was the beauty of the gesture of your hand.

You surrounded my body with light, such was the light of your eyes.

Husband. Take my hand.

We'll rise, we'll be a single god in the sky.

My roundness in your arms made that god's geometry die. We burn flowers to burn God.

You can't withstand me. Feel us, then try to even remember your god who had no face or voice or name or skin.

I will have you. I'll unfold a universe through you.

You'll be the planet I love best. Out of all those burnt or frozen planets, you alone will tan, heat through, blossom.

Your skin will flower out, grow a billion fingering vines, intoxicating berries, sticky-hearted foods that won't know death.

You subscribed to stone, you worshiped the permanent. But our male child will be more powerful than the permanent. He'll inhale winds and exhale oceans. The paths he'll make through the air will be gone as he makes them. The paths he makes in the water will be trackless. His movement will live in our eyes, we'll love to watch him.

I subscribed to your god, to stone, I worshipped the eternal. But our female child will live like a sun that rises and never sets. The love on her face will be eternity, set into eyes that see. Her heart will stop time.

Our children will live.

Oh, love. Walking around alone, annihilating ourselves with yearning, we wrapped our bodies in our iron chains. Now they're liquid silver on our skin.

That god was in you, begging you to break him open.

While I dissolved him, while he thanked me for his death, I let him know my name. I am she who was here before he was born. I know the heart of every beast of the ground who ever trembled in desperation, feeling my thumb on its spine as I pressed it into the heat of its mate.

To live forever is to be very young, because your life is endlessly ahead.

I am not Egypt, or Nile, or God, or Dimeter, or the seeds I make writhe and break open, or the flowers I burn to ash.

Since seeing your face I live in a continuous explosion, consuming myself.

I will destroy you in me. You're very old, but you'll never reach the land of the dead.

Your god is in powder, scattered across the world.

He's fallen through your fingers. Come to me.

I'm your mate. Come to me.

The desert is eternally wide. Come find my eyes.

The night is eternally long. You have time to reach a finger into my mouth, and stop the moon.

I'm giving myself to you. The rest of the world will pine for me. I'll love them but I'll touch only you.

If other gods play viols to attract me, I'll speak kindly to them in the voice of strings. They'll never break through soft strings to touch me.

If other gods sing to me that I am radiant and delectable and have trans-

formed their spirit with my eyes, I'll raise my hand and reflect moon into their faces so that they gently forget.

We are not only our bodies. You will bleed from your sex, and I'll hymn in a deep voice. Trust me infinitely, and come to me tonight.

In every grain of the desert is heat that draws down the sky, begs it to sink right into the earth.

I will lie across this entire desert for you.

Dip down upon me. Touch here, don't hesitate. All of your god is in me; let me place it into you.

Let me worship your breath.

Let me press my head into your chest, and feel myself turn into you. Never forget me.

Take my hips in your hands, and make the future of this world. Never, never forget me.

Come paint lines on my face in your blood. A line down my chin for strength, curves under my eyes for ferocity. A line up my forehead for flight of thoughts. Spiral circling my neck to lift voice upward when we start to sing ourselves off this planet.

I'll write texts on your back in my blood, my eyes very close to your skin, painting each letter with a badger's hair, tiny. I'll write about the man who was incarnated as a rat because all he'd mastered was loneliness. This text will protect you from loneliness.

In the end we'll live in flames together.

In flames our fear will melt and settle across the tops of our hearts like flowing bronze.

You'll drink my bronze fear, it'll scorch your body and blacken the core of you. I'll watch your face in its wounding, and your loving eyes will just deepen for me, till I cry. And I'll drink your molten fears away. In my mouth they'll be honey wine, fig wine.

We'll breathe flame and it'll be blue light in our nostrils, the immolation of the world. The scorching will be hearts-pain. I'll hear your breath catch as you touch my burning shoulder with the palm of your burning hand.

Your breath caught when I first looked at you.

You were scared. You remembered your church and your peaceful death in stillness, cool darkness. With no need to love, nothing to feel. With all your hopelessness and calm.

You tried to evaporate away from me. You rose through my arms as mist, and vanished.

Saying, I must
And God's Truth
And Peace

But you're my life. If you turn to a cloud, I'll follow as a cloud.

If you turn against love, I'll turn against love, I love you that much.

If you run from me, if you forget me, then I'll sit with my feet in the pond and think nothing. If nothing is infinite within you, then I'll be nothing, filling you eternally.

That day you walked around the outside of the house of God, holding your head in your hands. Your voice praised his name, but your mind wanted me, heard my voice, felt my heat. God is infinite, and my life is so small. You hold it between your two hands. This torture is very small. I am only a girl. See if you can defeat me.

Try and peel me from your skin. Even if you have to peel your own skin off.

Dump oceans of words on this red flame. Sing every song about pain that makes your pain decrease.

I saw you singing "Girl of the red river" and you suddenly leaned against a stone wall. No hymn to God can rack you like a simple love song everybody sings cheerfully, an easy song about pain.

If death is infinite, the pain of our being separate would be twice infinite. If your dissolved God was eternal, then we're eternally more than eternal.

Because he was the god of the withheld caress he moved above the waters. But he was not the goddess of the water. The goddess had a body, and when she spilled herself into the dry earth in a voluptuary river of swirling blood, and she was guzzled by the groaning earth, and she spread her body out as she sank down, sighing, when she gave herself to the earth in joy, God, watching, was unprepared for the gasp that stopped his breath.

Put your hand on my breast. You're holding the heart of music, the heart of the apple, the heart of the river. the heart of milk.

Your desert god was a spirit of sand, of glare, of dust. Put your hand on my thigh. Here in your hand is the soul of bees, the sex of nectarines, the belly of hummingbirds, the lips of lambs.

But we won't be Heaven together, where life ends. We'll be Eden, the place time begins. Here in your hand is the womb of the earth's core, here's the first landscape. My scent is the first wind that ever blew.

Beauty will want to drink us dry. Look, you abandoned me in the desert. I could have wept, but I drank God down and sat drunk on the ground, running my hands over the fertile fuckable earth.

A priest's name was Spek but that boundary breaks open.

Now his surrender overflows the desert.

His submission breaks the walls that surround the world.

It drowns the sky.

The whole world-ocean of yearning, and you only have to take a single droplet and put it to your lips.

All persons who aren't us will be stones at the bottom of the ocean.

All will sink, all will drown without ever feeling you wash across their bodies.

All gods will be silent symbols carved into the rocks undersea.

Oh beloved, you're here with me, the flood gushing from your eyes. You created white light in ocean form. It burns, shrivels, turns ashes to flesh, turns laws to spirit.

Alone, my husband, the one who needs all.

And he hears my voice say, love, drink one drop of this milk.

Here on my finger.

Here, look closely. It's an ocean. Under the milk are suns, gods, time. I drowned the universe with milk, it was an accident. All I said was, Please, but the word never stopped coming from my mouth, then it poured from my eyes, then it poured from my breasts.

Then even the innocent were desired to death. Their scattered eyes all looked into my face at once, they forgot their sandals and carts and hair and wine and lambs, they became needles passing through the center of love.

Breadselling woman, you'll die of how gently your grey braided hair moves in the sun.

Dog, you'll die of how passionately you snuffle and scratch at the temple door.

Peddler of brass plates, the rock has been struck with rock, the dead click has sounded. Your love is bent within you, it will rip you as it desperately expands.

Woman who is the sandstone-seller's wife, the pulsing you feel in your belly when you see the slave girl pass, that is your path, follow it into my mouth.

Qurratulain, visitor to Egypt, says: no end, no end to beauty. Your need is the weight of a mountain within you. Your fate is the thin grey smoke rising from the incense, that looks like rope for you to climb to safety, until just the thought of a breeze tumbles and shivers it into spirals. Spirals cut into the air can stop your breath, they return your need to you, return, return.

We'll lie deep in the white milkflowers. I'll catch a petal and press it to your lips, and feel it melt into honey as my finger pets you there.

I'll catch a leaf falling and press it to your chest, and it too was honey, it melts as my palm brushes you there.

I find a bird's egg in the flowers and I press it to your sex, press until it breaks, and it was full of honey, I swirl it into you.

Mead and frothed milk will fill your head with heat, you'll toss your head with your eyes closed, you won't know if the earth is under or beside or atop you.

What you want is what you are, you're the red water that breaks the riverbank and roars out of control attacking the ordered places of the world, and destroys and changes all landscape so the earth is never the same, and red trees grow from the new black delta mud that's squirming with creatures never before seen

and each tree has a million leaves, and each leaf is shaped like wings, redder than deep-in-your-body red

and if you come near the leaf with your finger, it'll wrap around you, you'll fall in love, you'll be lost to the world

because I love you, husband, and I've been wrapped with a million honey leaves

and the love I was born with was flooded by floods of stronger love, and those have been obliterated by love that's stronger still

until I'm only this

the womb you seek

the earth melting us together

promising softness

whispering till we're infinite softness

the first rock, where life first squirmed and sought other life, now shattered by this wave

a thousand armories, swords and hard bucklers and the shields worn by important men, clattering and tumbling in the red river together with cookpots and donkey harnesses and barrel hoops, all getting polished brighter and brighter till they can't remember the name of the enemy.

If you press into me till we're the same person, then I'll die. You'll have to create me again, you, the only creating being. You'll have to explode me out of air and light in your hands, as you've done every day since we first created the world together.

You say you didn't know. But you knew.

The turmoil around your chest, the anguish that made any hollow spot in creation an ache to you. You knew. You knew what wind and thunder meant.

Your belly glowed with lettering in the shapes of birds, of snakes.

You knew.

Let's go where death doesn't go, and distribute our joy among every creature.

And set up a wedding arch made of the dreams of beasts with fur, and marry our touch within the flesh of the mango.

And marry our minds in the sex of the honeysuckle, marry our time by lifting mountains, so all shadows stand still.

We'll speak the old words.

When you created light you spoke that tongue.

I was the light you created.

What did you think would happen when you turned the ocean over? You slid into my mouth with your fingers. How could I fold myself down like a storybook, and fit calmly into your pocket?

You turned me into a river. Could I square myself off into dry tiles of flood?

When you pull down a mountain, it buries you in your need.

You laid your whole body onto my tongue so I could call to you.

You invented words just so you could hear me whisper.

You gave me every word at once, and complete freedom. And the first words I said to you were,

Let us climb in our boat and bring the sun across the waters of time.

In wonder at your own creating hand, you stepped into a boat that didn't exist till I set its liquid name on your tongue.

Your feet rested on the word I spoke, "boat." The air of the planet suddenly had to remember a whole history of trees, so your feet could feel wood. When you looked at my hair and saw a gold crown there, the earth groaned, now pregnant with soft metals. A human race called itself from nothing, just so two mammal hands could have gripped and turned and hammered my crown and set faience and turquoise and rosewood into its band.

You spoke without looking down at the earth. Your first words forgot yourself. You created accidentally, gazing at me.

You told me: Pour out the sky for our boat to travel.

Those words created my past. My memory lit up now, I saw when I first captured the sky. It was the size of a mind then, I remembered, it frothed and swirled as I caught it blue in my two hands.

You created my body at that moment, as a bottle to capture sky in. I poured it down into myself and closed my mouth and held the sky till you would appear.

You created my yearning then, a sky that rushed through my blood, trying to fill empty space, but always there was more empty space in me. So the gusting of the sky throughout me never stopped.

You created time in its tormenting slowness then, so I could remember lying awake feeling my chest desperate for calm, feeling my shoulders want to die, destroy themselves, to eat trees and knock down walls to find calm.

Pour out the sky *you said,* a river for our boat. *And you made river have its meaning, you soaked the skins of all the tribes while you looked in my eyes. I was a river as I opened my mouth.*

Then time in its circling was born, as a river flowed out of me and embraced us, filling all the directions. Sky never stopped flowing, and seemed still. Sky rushed up my legs, and my restlessness was soothed, my desire to jump off the world was calmed. Sky left my belly, so I wasn't tormented by the rrrwrrr belly, the swirling need. Sky blew out of my chest, so I didn't feel desperate, about to explode.

The sky was a settled form of time, gazing down on us, waiting.

And you still only gazed at my face.

You could see me. Light existed.

A sun.

You hung a flame in the sky, just as a lantern to see my face. Just to show me your face yearning.

Light, insane floods of light.

I looked down and saw who I am to you. My bare feet on flower petals, bare body illuminated. Standing in our boat clothed only in a gold crown.

Your own crown of lapis and white hammered silver, it blinded me.

Upon our crowns, across them both, rested the entire sun in all its finality.

The light was thought-destroying, world-vaporizing.

Light so total it shone through our bones.

You were staring mystified into my spiraling dark excessive hair. In this light the need behind your eyes burned me.

You saw song in my fingers. So I held them up and fretted the air.

You saw the sun-illumined wishes in my mind, and I poured them all on to the deck of the boat, so your feet could cool in my thought.

More than any mortal lovers, we had light to see the other's face.

And desire for me pulled you.

We created the workings of the world then.

Desire pulled your thighs toward my thighs.

Desire pulled at your hips and arms, as you gazed at my bright molten belly.

Desire pulled your mouth and eyes and heart and mind into me.

Your desire pulled our boat out of its mooring, and we rose together, slowly, through the narrow gate of the sky, slowly across the river sky.

Now that we know desire moves the sun across the sky, we know everything.

Below us I saw all the pullings and pushings and creations of man. I saw the inner heavings of mountains. I saw every bird that flocks and follows.

I stared at you. I was staring into light.

You are the desire that pulls at every drop of the seas.

You are what pulls the Nile itself from south to north.

You are why the waters flood across the two lands, and leave the earth writhing.

You told me, you spoke it. I understood, because your face was so certain.

You said: It's you. You have always existed.

Because I'm the sun. You named me, and out of the endless explosion of my name I poured perpetual heat back into your blood.

I inhale the black space, I exhale the breath of every needy lover. Every creature is a lover, every one.

Hydrogen to enflame you, helium to exalt you.

I'll sing heat across this terrible space between us. I'll wrap fire around your waist.

You created me and you don't realize.

You think that by losing your religion, you were only a man who dove off a high cliff into the waters of the sea. You think you dove as a man dives, just to try to impress one girl on that crowded beach.

You dreaded hearing female laughter as you fell through sunlight, knowing that would kill you in mid-air.

You fell through the air soaked in embalming hopelessness, like a body in natron, like one whose organs, set in jars, are separated in a small stone place.

Because you lived in humility and longing, you only imagine one humiliating death.

Yet you dove, it was worth your life to make the gaze of one ancient young girl turn to love.

As you fell, you said to that girl: I've spent too much time on the earth, please take my life and throw it into the ocean

     please:

     let me dive doubled-over, clutching my middle, overcome with the sex
of the sea

     let the dive continue after I enter the water

     let me reach the bottom of all and imprint my belly in the deepest
sand

     let me drown and shudder and become the motion of the waves

     let me feel the pull downward downward, let me feel the chaos of my
body when the drinking sea transforms it, let the moon stretch me out into a
river under the sea

     let me forget the squared footpaths of cities and the orderly language
of men

     let me become the liquid that writhes within life

     and from the uncanny heat in me let the seabed crack open

     let the waters fall down into the hollow earth

     let me spiral into the red core of earth

     let me touch the center of this life

     and become one drop of what makes life continuous

     and be sweated onto the surface of the earth, myself, one drop

     instantly destroyed by your heat, beloved sun

     exhaled by earth as mist, inhaled by you as your rightful breath.

     You, sun over Egypt. Ra surrounds you. Jesus surrounds you. The
mother of earth surrounds you.

     Your hand shines on the manuscripts of the East. You light the blue
eyes and the brown eyes.

     You're our power in the sky, your life is poured out for its gorgeous-
ness.

Consume this body.

I waved my life away with a gesture, I told my life, "go." But that gesture is for your mouth to eat.

Your double, your Ba, breathe it into my nostrils. Put your mouth over my face, and exhale yourself into me. Your beautiful water-tinted Ba will fly as a bird to my heart.

And take. Breathe my own Ba, let me gasp it into you. Inhale everything I am, hold and protect me in your chest. Let that be our only breath, the gasps that transfer our whole selves.

Let your skin be the sheath for my life.

We'll carry each other's selves safe within us all across the sky. If there were Ma'at then balance would be pleased; if Aether owned the upper air, he would smile at us. If there were Jesus then compassion would be pleased, order would be appeased if there were God.

I'll hold your double close within me. I'll finally understand your heart.

And you won't know which of us is speaking, but husband, but wife, I know. You sing out of my mouth, I can taste your tongue in this song. I sing my deepest voice out of your pale throat.

The words we sing are true as soon as they touch the air.

My mirror I pour into you. My personhood, my image, I pour down into you, to live there.

And without my desolated image to sink me, I rise. Without my traitorous image to drop me from the sky, I can never fall.

And your image in me, your flame—here in my chest—low in my throat—it's burning honey, it is peachtrees in flames.

It burns out the place where I breathed the common air. I no longer have speech to show others. Shining promises can no longer enter my chest. I

141

can no longer be found in the graven lists of men. I no longer show in the fire-painted rolls of women.

Instead I ring continuously.

I'm hollow, I ring like a flame burns, roaring never stopping.

It's you. I tell you the pain is nothing. This loss is infinitely beautiful. This destruction is perfect.

I tell you I'll keep you here, swallowed, burning, I'll protect you from any harm, all across our voyage on the waters.

When you speak gently to me, you speak out of my own chest. When I sing infinite love to you, my song comes from your throat.

We have been since the beginning of this.

I am eternal, we are eternal, you are eternal.

Let clay jars hold the organs of those who are wept over. No eyes can see us now.

The Ka of Spek, shadow of the desert saint, beloved of God, has fled, his shadow has fled the world. There's no shadow in this sunsoaked boat.

The Ka of Qurratulain, shadow of the sungoddess, lives not even within her. Her shadow is not even within her. Within her is the illuminated temple. Within her is all light.

I hold the sun in my arms, and I'm not annihilated by her.

I embrace the man I destroy and exalt and enflame.

This ceaseless explosion, this obliterating roar, this, this, us.

Where the body hovers in sweetness at the top of the spiral, and the touch of a finger would make mortal lovers fall through a thousand oceans of sweet dying—here our touch never makes us fall. We hover and tremble in continuing almost.

Oh heat in all desires.

Oh sun in the pull, sun in the lodestone, sun in human eyes.

Womb who is time, and continuation, and the vortex

Sun who's yourself and myself

Miracle who pours us, who makes us both miracles of giving.

I am your voice, I am the woman of your womb, I am the man who is your messenger, your messenger!

Exalted and enflamed, illumined and ecstatic, dead and undying, in song and in light, invisible and absolute, as wind, as darkness, in balance and careening

Almost destroyed in you, almost exploded in us, entwined in the explosion that doesn't end or begin

Always discovering you, always dreaming you, beloved archangel, dearest utter infinite goddess

Lit by the belly and lit by the mind, our soul the shape of our eyes, our soul the shape of our tenderly touching feet

I'm yours, I'm your husband, I'm your wife, even if it destroys the whole world, I am your messenger, your messenger.

Let there be a holocaust of us, let our apocalypse come. In destruction we'll find all we created in the beginning.

I'll be there in you, you in me, each uncountable particle still alive in us.

Each particle made of desire, each fragment orbiting its need, flying around each other hopelessly attracted, hopelessly desiring, maddened with heat and electricity, insane with the vision, insane with vehemence, insane with the arousal of embrace.

Burn, obliterate, melt, dazzle, use every power! My boiled-out heart flutters, I drop to the floor of the boat, and you're above me. This heat is the culmination of millions of years coming to a point, here, here. Destroy me again, destroy us again.

We've spoken these words out of each other's hearts since the time you began time.

Since the beginning we've felt this.

And late tonight, as always, love, we'll reach the darkness, we'll gently cool, infinitely old, and hide again behind the earth

and as always I'll whisper to you

we'll laugh secretly together and again the moon will catch our laughter and reflect it to the earth as love and mystery

and tomorrow morning you'll say to me

in a young voice

a new voice

the voice I love best of all:

Let us climb in our boat and bring the sun across the waters of time.

www.ingramcontent.com/pod-product-compliance
Lightning Source LLC
Chambersburg PA
CBHW081205170626
46813CB00010B/3328